Women Up On Blocks

Women Up On Blocks

STORIES

MARY AKERS

Press 53
Winston-Salem, North Carolina

Press 53
PO Box 30314
Winston-Salem, NC 27130

First Edition

Cover design by Kevin Watson
Cover photo, "Legs and Engines," Copyright © 2009 by Jenn Rhubright

Epigraph from "Rabbit Hole," Copyright © 2004 by Laura Kasischke,
from the book *Gardening in the Dark* (Ausable Press),
used by permission of the artist.

Stories in this collection have been published as follows: "Medusa Song" in
RE:AL The Journal of Liberal Arts, in the anthology *To Be Read Aloud*, and in *R-KV-R-Y*; "Animo, Anima, Animus" (forthcoming) in *Primavera*; "Wild, Wild
Horses" in *Literary Mama* (named a Notable Story by storySouth); "Mooncalf"
in *Compass Rose*; "Multicolored Tunneled Life" in *Wisconsin Review* and also in *R-KV-R-Y*; "Pygmalion (Recast) in *The Fiddlehead*; "Model Home" in *Ink Pot* and
also in *Literary Potpourri*; "The Rashomon Tree" in *Bellowing Ark*; "Wholesale"
in *Ars Medica*; "No Reason Not To" in *Fried Chicken and Coffee*; "Evangeline" in
To Be Read Aloud (winner of their 2008 Southern Writers' Award); and "Still Life
with Shoes" in *The Awakenings Review*.

Printed on acid-free paper

ISBN 978-0-9816280-6-6

Full of love, made of lies. The lies
were like a lot of shiny pins
sticking the self that wasn't me
to the one I could have been.

— Laura Kasischke

Contents

medusa song

She scrambles the eggs while the baby howls at her knees. To drown out the racket, she hums as she jabs her fork into the yolks. She enjoys the way they spill their yellow color and swirl into the whites. She matches her tune to the schook, schook, schook of the fork against the bowl, then does a quick sidestep when the baby lunges for her legs.

His little fat hands grasp the air, throwing him off balance. He totters on his heels for a moment then sits hard and rolls back sideways, bumping his head on the floor. He stops crying abruptly and flails his arms in the air like a big bug stuck on its back.

Cynthia knows she should pick him up, comfort him, but she's too deep in her own need. She won't look down, even, because if she looks at his face all twisted up and desperate for her, she'll have to pick him up, and she just can't do that motherhood stuff right now.

She used to love the feeling, everyone needing her so badly. She would peel and seed John's oranges when she packed his lunch. She cut the crusts off his sandwich out of pure love. And when the baby fell asleep, she'd sit and hold him just as long as he would sleep.

But John Junior is walking now—into everything—and he's gotten so clingy. Her friend Alice says that John Junior is feeling separation anxiety. Every time Cynthia leaves the room he thinks she's gone forever, just disappeared. Secretly, Cynthia wishes it could work like that—two steps into the bedroom, and poof, she's in another life, another world.

She used to love her life. She looked forward to every day. Cynthia can't even say when things changed. Maybe it was back when she suspected John of sleeping with his secretary. Maybe it was after John Junior was born and she couldn't seem to do anything right.

John and she had never fought before. Well, sometimes, but it was always more of a disagreement and once Cynthia apologized it would be over. It never spilled out into the rest of her life.

Now things seem to get all tangled up, till she can't separate them, one from the other. She feels like that woman with snakes for hair, only all her problems are tangled up there too, squirming and writhing around, hissing on top of her head.

She figures that must be why John isn't home yet—imagine living with a woman who can't comb her hair for the snakes. She tries calling his office, but that snooty Angela answers, so Cynthia puts on a different voice and pretends to be one of John's clients.

"Mr. Albee promised to show us a home today, is he in?"

She smiles because she knows Angela is too dense to figure out it's her. She's careful to keep the smile out of her voice.

Then Angela says, "Mr. Albee hasn't been in all day, Ma'am, may I give him a message?"

She says it real sly-like, with extra emphasis on the ma'am, until Cynthia is really getting sick. The eggs look disgusting and she feels so nauseous. Then she's throwing up again, retching in the toilet, and thinking, God, please don't let me be pregnant, but she's known it for a while. Add another snake.

When she's wiping her face, John calls and she thinks he says he's at work, but it's hard to hear for sure over the baby. Liar. She just called there. Cynthia doesn't want to yell at him, but she feels it rising up in her throat like bile, and she wants to stop it but the words are pouring out all over the place like vomit, sour and steaming.

She hangs up and tries to finish supper, even if it is just eggs and toast. After John sells a house they'll have steak. She puts the baby in his crib, and over the monitor she can hear him banging his head against the bars. She goes to the door and watches, fascinated. His eyes roll back in pleasure. She tries banging her own head once on the doorframe before she remembers the snakes. No sense getting them all riled up.

Then she hears the eggs frying too hard, and sure enough, they're brown when she stirs them, and the toast needs scraping. Schook, schook, schook, the crumbs fly all over the sink, sticking to the sides. She thinks about that woman who drove her kids into the lake and cried about it on national TV. What a terrible person, a horrible mother. But the snakes hiss, "Yessss."

She's barely gotten the toast buttered when John Junior starts up again. He's poopy, too. She can see it rimming the edges of his diaper. What with the snakes and the baby it's really all just too much for her and she carries him out to the pickup and puts him squish onto the seat and she leaves supper unfinished and she's really going to do it this time because she just can't take it any more.

Halfway to the lake it starts raining. John Junior is sitting in the floorboard playing with his toes and the wipers are keeping time in the dark, schook, schook, schook, marking off the seconds till it's done.

Cynthia pulls right up to where the lake meets the road, and there's no one around, so she gets out and goes over to the water's edge. The baby watches her, his face against the window, nose flattened, big eyes shining white through the dark.

The water smells dank and fishy and it's way too cold when she sticks her head in. Cynthia is on all fours holding her breath and she thinks about how she must look—rear in the air, head in the lake. She doesn't get up, though, and her chest starts to ache from needing to breathe. Her head is throbbing, and her throat spasms, her body trying to force her to breathe. But she won't, she won't, and she can hear the schook, schook, schook of blood in her head, looking for oxygen.

Just when her body starts to relax and she's feeling like she could stay down there at the bottom of the lake forever, she jerks her head up hard, throwing back her shoulders, landing on her back at the muddy edge of the lake.

And possibly the baby is crying in the truck, but he's safe enough, and she remembers that his diaper needs changing while she watches drops of rain fall silver through the night and feels them sting her cold lake-water face as she listens and waits and hopes the snakes have drowned.

animo, anima, animus

J enny lines up the seams by their notches, pushing the shaggy synthetic fur to the inside as she sews. She presses her foot hard against the pedal on the old Singer and the needle struggles through the thick fabric, katack, katack, katack, while the motor gives off a smell like burning rubber. The boom box, resting on the wide headboard of her bed, blasts out a Barenaked Ladies CD and she moves her shoulders in time to the music, chair-dancing and singing as she works. When the seam is done she turns it inside out—a perfect tiger's ear. The ear, and its mate, will be attached to a plastic headband and worn tomorrow, along with brown and orange greasepaint stripes, and nothing else.

In many ways, working the cage beats stripping—there's less work and greater public exposure, especially when she makes the papers, which she pretty much always does—but it's also a chillier job, outside, on the street, and she gets cramped staying in one huddled spot for so long. Of course she knows it's nothing compared to what those poor animals must feel their whole lives, and that's part of why she does it, too.

Jenny stays abreast of the information. She keeps current, even though the stories upset her: the zoo that kept a violent male bear with a female bear even though he repeatedly attacked her and eventually killed her in front of a group of school children; the

Jesse Helms constitutional amendment that says rats and mice are not animals and so can be experimented on, repeatedly cutting them open and sewing them back up without anesthesia; the testing of household cleaners by pouring them into rabbits' eyes and keeping detailed records of the systematic destruction; newborn chimpanzees ripped from their mothers' arms and given to human parents to raise in trailers in New Mexico . . . these things are hard to live with. It's why she does what she does.

Jenny thinks about tomorrow and decides that she'll pick one person from the leering crowd—a man, most likely—who looks a little less than comfortable and really bore her eyes into him like the tiger she's supposed to be. She could add it to her dramatic resume as *character acting* or maybe *mime*, although miming isn't really a respectable gig anymore.

But the cage! The cage gives her the same thrill as a strip club runway surrounded by drink-happy, money-waving men, with the added bonus of raising awareness about mistreated animals, of course. Jenny likes to do altruistic things—she's a softie, really—and loves animals. She'd always meant to take up a cause, ever since she was a little girl, but she'd never been very good at organizing things. Fortunately, though, nakedness has a way of getting people's attention all on its own, and she likes that. There's nothing quite like the burning eyes of men, running all over your body, to make you feel alive.

Most women didn't *get* men. They thought men wanted only women with perfect bodies and that they noticed things like dimpled cellulite thighs and thick ankles. But Jenny knows that what men notice is nakedness. Skin, pure and simple. And after that, they notice T & A, any size or color, the bigger the better, usually. Fortunately Jenny has plenty of both. Some belly, too, but not enough to be gross—more of a soft/sexy Marilyn Monroe thing. Besides, Jenny's found that if you act like you think you're gorgeous, you are. Especially when you're naked.

Of course, Matt, Jenny's lover, hates to see her in the cage. He has to leave before she even gets out of her robe at the start, if he goes at all. He especially can't be there when the street is full of men eating hot dogs and drinking coffee, ogling her and making comments. Matt's mid-way through his Navy Seal training, at Dam Neck, Virginia, and says the cage makes him crazy, makes him want to grab his rifle and start shooting into the crowd. Which, as far as Jenny is concerned, is another really good thing about doing it.

Matt always forgives her afterwards, though, especially when she puts on heavy red lipstick, pushes her cleavage up and sings, "Happy Birthday, Mr. President" to him, with a slow, pouty, throatiness.

As she sews the finished ear onto the headband, she sings along with her favorite song on the whole CD: *If I Had a Million Dollars.* The line about buying a fur coat—but not a real fur coat!—is her favorite. She loves their music. She'd be happy to strip for the Barenaked Ladies if she could, just to give them back a little something, since their music has made her so happy and validated her life's path.

What would Jenny buy if she had a million dollars? A wild, multicolored shoulder tattoo, the best she could get. Then she'd give $50,000 to PETA and the SPCA, right off, without batting an eye. Jenny used to think she'd get something pierced if she had money, but now that she's almost 22 she realizes that piercing's a cheap thing to do to your body, and the one thing she doesn't want to be is cheap.

⌘

Andrea drives across town, heading for another long day at the sweat factory. The Sweat Factory. It sounds so brutal and harsh, when in fact, they just make sweats. But fifteen years of feeding the same damned zipper over and over through the machine had begun to wake Andrea in the night with shooting wrist pains and numbness in her fingers. Even holding the car's steering wheel was getting painful. Maybe her supervisor could switch her to a different department. Maybe if she made 750 drawstring eyelets a day, instead, her wrists would ease up on her.

The early morning sun casts a glare across her windshield and makes her wish she'd brought her sunglasses. Her head throbs. She must've had one too many last night, but who's counting? She'll drink a big glass of water with an aspirin when she gets to work, and be ready to face the day, same as ever. Andrea hadn't missed a day of work in three years. Whatever else could be said about her, there was always that.

She turns her head and stares as she drives past a group of placard-toting protestors. They stand around a sign for the circus, chanting something she can't decipher. They look young and angry, but she can't think why anyone would picket something as wholesome and all-American as a circus. The Greatest Show on Earth. Man. How long had it been since she'd gone to something like that? Since childhood, for sure. She is hit with the sudden memory of sparkly blue cotton candy crystals sticking to her fingers, wet from licking, and the barker calling out a waltzing line of elephants, tail-to-trunk in exotic tasseled headpieces. What a sight.

None of her three ex-husbands had cared a whit for that sort of thing, and she'd had no kids, so there hadn't been a reason to go for all these years. But now she thinks she'd like to, and she thinks Ricky, her current husband, might like to go, too. They're more or less newlyweds, and have never really talked about the circus before—it just plain hadn't come up—but when she pictures Ricky, always wearing his ball cap, chewing big wads of watermelon bubble gum, and watching Saturday morning cartoons until noon, it makes her think he just might.

Being married was such a hard thing. There was so much adjustment, so much to learn. But it was also the most natural thing in the world. Every one of her husbands had driven her to near insanity with the pleasureful thrust and urge of anxious sex, and you couldn't deny *that* as the basis for a good marriage. But somehow, it hadn't kept the wolf from the door. Andrea's never figured that one out. She was a woman who would drop everything, anytime, anywhere, for good, hard loving. And she liked it, even. Surely it was every man's fantasy to have to stop supper and bend his hot wife over the table, into the spaghetti and meatballs. She can picture Ricky slurping the long red noodles off her breasts, lapping them up like a puppy.

Which is exactly what Ricky *is* like, a big old puppy, happy and open, and eager. It's why she married him. Because she's as serious as she can be about marriage and she wants this one to last.

⌘

Jenny fixes Matt his favorite dinner. Spaghetti and meatballs. Usually she leaves the meatballs out, or tries to make tofu ones, but it's the real deal tonight, because Matt loves meat and she needs him in a good mood. She hasn't told him yet about tomorrow's demonstration and she wants the discussion to go well.

"Wow, Jenzie, this is great," says Matt after slurping up a long noodle. "These, uh, whatchacallem, soyballs really taste like meat this time."

Jenny smiles and pulls a strand of hair from her ponytail, twisting it around her finger. The sauce bubbles on the stove, building up steam and exploding in small volcano bursts, spraying the perimeter of the burner with dark red droplets. She rises and stirs the pot, then flicks the burner off with a loud snap. She turns to Matt. "I'm in the cage tomorrow, Mattie," she says in a rush of words, then turns back to the pot, stirring vigorously. "It's a protest against the circus, this time, and you know how bad they are," she tells the steaming sauce.

"Outside?" says Matt, putting down his fork.

"Yes."

"When?"

"Noon-ish," Jenny says. She returns to the table but pushes her plate away and rests her elbows on the table. "It's really important. We can totally get the word out."

"I hate it when you do this. Stripping at the club is bad enough, but outside? And lunch time?" Matt shifts his plate a three-quarter turn. "What if one of my buddies or the C.O. sees?"

"Then maybe he'll join the cause," says Jenny, smiling.

"Cause," says Matt with a snort.

"It's a cause." Jenny crosses her arms and leans back. "A good one. And it's important, whether you believe it or not. Animal rights are coming, Matt. Pretty soon, a person who thinks people are better than animals will be a specieist, and it'll be as bad as being racist, or sexist. You wait and see. All we want are laws. On the books. Protecting animals."

"I know, I know. All the little innocent baby animals being killed for their fur."

"They live in wire cages, Matt. Their paws never touch the ground. They go mad from confinement and gnaw their flesh to the bone. They cannibalize their cage mates. They get killed by anal electrocution. What kind of life is that?"

"Uh, the life of an animal?"

"It doesn't have to be. It wasn't meant to be that way. It's brutal. And cruel. And—"

Matt grabs Jenny's hand and holds it firmly. "It's really great that you care so much, honey. It's sweet. You're sweet. If I were an animal, I'd want you on my side. But I'm not. And you know where I stand. I grew up hunting. I eat meat. I wear leather. And I try to understand how you feel, but I just don't get it. Not the way you do. I mean, animals were put here on earth for us. For us to use. They aren't people."

"True," she says, sitting forward and spitting the word out. "*They* only kill when they're hungry. People kill for sport. For pleasure. And by the way, animals don't make war on each other, either. Only people do that."

"Oh no? Bet they do." Matt drops her hand then points suddenly. "What about Army ants?"

"That's different—it's a territory thing."

"And rams that slam into each others' heads?"

"That's to win a mate."

"Well, that's what Navy Seals are trained to do, too. Defend territory and win a mate. We're animals."

"Very funny," Jenny says. She carries her plate to the sink and scrapes it into the disposal. "But you're not a Seal, yet."

⌘

Andrea's Friday shift is finally over. She takes a long drag on her first post-work cigarette, pulling the smoke into her lungs and exhaling slowly. People always thought she had such a soft job, working with fleece all day, but the shit went everywhere, clinging to her hair, her clothes, her eyelashes, going up her nose. She could fill a tissue with gobs of wet, red, fuzz, after breathing in the floating residue for ten hours straight.

By the time Ricky comes in from his mechanic's job at the Shell station by the shipyard, she's on her fourth beer, and her third cigarette. She's happy to see him. "Hey, baby." She raises the beer in salute. "Happy hour started early tonight."

"I see," he says, dropping his jacket. "Got one left for me?"

"Course. Got that, and more." She looks up at him and licks the bottle's rim.

"How is it you always get me hot?" Ricky says, bending over and reaching into the open fridge.

"It's your older woman complex. You like the sexy mother type."

"That so?" Ricky sits across from her at the table and kicks off his heavy steel-toed boots. The leather toe boxes are blackened by small soak stains of motor oil and drips of gasoline; the uppers are brown.

"Put them nasty things by the door," says Andrea. "P. U."

"Yes, Momma," says Ricky, saluting with his free hand, grinning.

"Hey," says Andrea, "you want to go see the circus?" Without waiting for his answer she continues. "It's in town. Tomorrow at noon. I saw the sign today. Just for fun. Whatdya think?"

⌘

Jenny's demonstration coordinator, Don, straightens her headband to center the ears, gives her a wink and helps her off with the terrycloth robe. He leads her over to the cage and opens its door. Her skin draws up in the cool air and begins to itch under the greasepaint. Don hooks the leather collar around her neck and clips it to the bars of the cage as she squats down and duck-walks in. There's no crowd yet, just an older couple who stare for a moment then look away quickly. Don padlocks the door with a final sounding click. The cold metal bars press into her feet. She wraps her arms around her bent knees and waits.

The first person to arrive is the hot dog vendor, pushing his rolling cart closer, either to watch, or sell to the spectators he anticipates. The creaking of the wheels seems unnaturally loud in the thin air of late morning. Jenny doesn't look up when he says hello. She tries to focus on what the tiger would be feeling, get inside that skin, see the world from inside those eyes.

⌘

Andrea is pretty sure Ricky just came to the circus to please her. He's got his hands deep in his pockets, a pinch in his lower lip, plus he yelled at the parking attendant when he had to pay three dollars to get into the lot.

"Thanks for coming, baby," she says, rubbing his arm as they stand in line. "I know Saturday's your only day off." He looks at her then, but doesn't say anything. "It'll be worth it. I promise."

"We even in the right line?" Ricky looks at the crowd around them.

"Sure, it's the right line, honey. It's just moving slow is all." At least she thinks it's the line for the circus. They're definitely outside the arena, and she can see the tents with their pointy tops and colorful flaps, but the line they're in doesn't seem to be moving.

"I don't know." Ricky lifts the ball cap on his head and repositions it. "I'm not sure."

"Okay. You keep our place," she tells him, "I'll see what's up." She moves around the clump of people and stops. "Oh, it isn't a line at all," she says loudly, calling back to him. "It's some sort of animal show. I can see the edge of a cage. Everybody's just watching."

"What animal is it?"

"All's I see is an ear, kind of brownish. It's not really moving or anything. Come on, let's find the entrance." Something doesn't feel right to Andrea and she wants to leave. The faces of the people standing around look strange, somehow. And they're all men, she suddenly realizes. "Let's go," she says, and grabs Ricky's arm, but he's clearly sensed something, too, and he pulls back.

"Just a sec," he says, craning his neck.

⌘

Jenny can feel the crowd closing in. She wonders when the police will show up. They always do. She's already made the papers for tomorrow, too. She sensed the reporter as soon as he showed up, walking quickly, all business, snapping pictures, then moving off.

The men who are left surround the cage wearing looks of happy disbelief, as if they've been granted a prize, seeing a naked woman in the middle of the day, unexpectedly, with no repercussions. Jenny can hear the comments of the closer men, tossed around for one another's benefit: "Who knew my lunch hour would be so interesting today?"

"Think I'll run away and join the circus. Tame me some tigers!"

"Whatsa matter honey? Cat got your tongue?"

"Meow!"

Jenny tries not to smile in her crouch. She loves men. Their needs are so simple, and they're so easily pleased. She could just hug them all. But she reminds herself that she has a purpose today, and so prepares her caged animal stare, a mixture of hurt puppy, scared kitten, and angry lion.

She looks up. The first man whose eye she catches grins and looks away quickly. The second one winks and clucks his tongue, rocking back on his heels. The third one, just emerging around the edge of the crowd, is different. He looks at her like he's got her figured out, has known her all his life. Her hairline prickles when she locks eyes with him. Then there's a half smile going between them, like a private joke. His bottom lip pouches out slightly, under a goatee, and he's wearing a blue CAT ball cap with the sides of the bill bent down, matching the angles of his face. He seems to know her. Maybe he's been to the club, but it bothers Jenny that she can't place him. She looks down for a moment, then back up.

There's a woman with him, Jenny sees that now. She's pulling at his arm, but he just keeps staring at Jenny with that half smile flickering around his lips, secretive-like.

The woman with him stops pulling. She's hard. It's a cliché, but a perfect one-word description. Her hair is long and brown, teased up and sprayed, with tiny yellow streaks in it. She's wearing tight jeans and a denim jacket. Her face has a yellowed, leathery appearance. Too many hours in the tanning salon, maybe, with the extra tinge of a chain-smoker. The hard woman watches the man in the ball cap as he watches Jenny.

⌘

Andrea sees now that it isn't an animal at all. It's a woman. And she isn't wearing any clothes, just some paint which hardly covers anything. She wonders what kind of circus would advertise itself with a naked woman. And what kind of woman would take the job. This certainly wasn't what she had in mind when she dragged Ricky out this morning. She had thoughts of trained poodles, and a lion tamer, and maybe a trapeze, with a girl in sparkling, scanty clothes who spins by her teeth, but not this.

The men are riveted, though. Ricky, too, and it's sickening. Andrea can't imagine how any woman could sell herself in this way, and be so cheap. She looks at the cage, and at the woman's legs, none too thin, she sees. The roots of her hair are dark and there are chill bumps visible under the body paint. Surely none of the men have noticed that. And she does look frightened, actually. Well, who wouldn't, naked in a cage, outdoors, surrounded by leering men?

Andrea's anger dissolves. She sees the sadness of the picture: a young woman, reduced to being no more than a naked body, surrounded by men who only want entertainment, at her expense. Andrea is not a feminist by any means, and doesn't want to be one, but this scene makes the back of her throat swell with pity.

⌘

Even as she stares at the sexy fellow in the baseball cap, Jenny is aware of the woman beside him. That woman isn't happy, and who can blame her? Her man is digging Jenny in a major way. And Jenny is totally into the way his stare makes her feel. It's as if his presence has transformed her into the tiger she's portraying. She can feel her muscles loosening, sliding beneath her skin, her legs lengthening, longing to run, her jaws salivating. She has a vision of wetly prowling through a mangrove swamp, of red flesh ripped from its silver sinews, of delicate foot bones cracking beneath her back teeth.

But the woman's eyes bring Jenny back to the moment. She's older than the man, sad-looking, probably desperate. Jenny gets a strong feeling as she watches this dark-eyed woman watch her man watch Jenny. It's a feeling that Jenny thinks will alter her life from here on out. The feeling that she, Jenny, may be the one squatting in a cage, but this hard woman is spending her days staring out between the bars of her own sad cage, one she built all by herself, one she'll probably die in.

Jenny looks away then, and deliberately empties her mind. She will not interfere. It would be ridiculous, anyway, to think that something, anything, could come of a chance encounter, on a sidewalk, in a cage.

wild, wild horses

"Put it in gear," Paul yelled from the rear of the car.

"I'm trying," Missy called back, over the noisy rattle of the engine. Her hands began to sweat; she could feel the gears resisting, grinding slightly as she pressed the gearshift into what she thought was reverse. Paul's '65 Mustang shuddered beneath her and she wiped her palms, one at a time, on her pants.

"Just push it," Paul yelled. "Hard!"

So she did. And it sounded like two cats in the midst of a brawl being sprayed with buckshot. "Shit," she said under her breath as the gearshift popped back out. She hated helping Paul with his restoration projects, and she had shed more blood over this vehicle than she cared to admit. Like the time she scraped her knuckles nearly to the bone holding onto the rear convertible lift while Paul hit the button up front and called out, "Don't let go, whatever you do." She hadn't. Even when her skin did.

"Christ, just slide over. I'll get it up there myself," Paul said, suddenly beside her.

Slide over, a difficult thing to do with front bucket seats, but she scrambled past the gearshift to sit in the passenger's side, feeling as if she had failed some crucial wifeliness test. But then working with Paul always made her feel that way, as if she should know, instinctively, the appearance and use of a strap wrench. As if she

17

should study up, in her spare time, in order to be the perfect automotive scrub nurse to his grease monkey surgeon.

The car bucked up the garage incline then lurched to a stop just short of the back wall.

"I don't know how you make it stop just right," Missy said. "I'm always sure I'll send it shooting back through the wall and into the living room."

"No big deal," Paul said, appeased by her praise. "It's like riding a horse. You feel it underneath you. It responds. You respond to it. Piece of cake." He clapped her on the shoulder, buddy-like.

"Sure," she said. "Piece of cake. What're you working on?"

"Got to get the rear wheels off and take out the coil springs, then put in heavy-duty ones from the junkyard. I'll jack it up and put a stand under each axle. Poor man's lift."

"Can you do that all by yourself?"

"Sure. No problem. Won't take any time at all."

"All right. Well, I should go in." She glanced at the watch on her wrist. "The girls are probably done with their tape. I left Hannah in the walker with an ear of corn-on-the-cob." She opened the car door and looked back. "Teething," she added, to answer Paul's questioning look.

"Okay, sure," said Paul. "Thanks, hon."

She stepped into the house in time to see the little mermaid kissing Eric happily-ever-after. King Triton swept up on a wave of his own making to get a kiss from Ariel, too, and Missy's throat constricted with emotion. Stupid Disney movies. She could always be counted on to tear up at all the right places. Conditioned, she was, just like Pavlov's dogs.

Two-year-old Jessica sat on her knees before the TV, much too close to the screen, bouncing slightly. Her fine brown hair had an ugly snarl in the back that Missy hadn't noticed this morning. There was always so much to stay on top of as a parent—long dirty fingernails, tangled hair, sugary teeth, potty breaks, car seats, hot things, hungry stomachs, electrical outlets. The list was endless, and the vigilance exhausting.

"You need to go potty?" Missy asked.

"Uh-huh," Jessica said, jumping up and running towards the bathroom. Missy noted the wet spot in the middle of Jessica's pink, ruffled shorts and felt the carpet where she had been sitting. Wet. She retrieved a towel from the linen closet and dropped it down then stepped on it with her full weight to encourage sopping.

Ten-month-old Hannah slept in her walker, shoulders and head slumped over sideways, her upper gums propped on the ear of corn, her mouth slack and drooling.

"I went potty, Mommy," said Jessica as she re-entered the room, elastic shorts cranked sideways around her middle.

"Did you flush?"

"Uh-huh."

"And wash?" Missy asked, leaning over to readjust the shorts.

"Yes."

"Let me smell."

Jessica held her arms out, fingers clenched. Missy sniffed, then said, "Go wash, Jessie," swatting her bottom with the tips of her fingers as Jessie squealed toward the bathroom. "You can help me cook when you're done," Missy called out, then heard the water running in the sink, accompanied by Jessie's hand-washing song.

The little details of her children's lives—that was what Missy was sure she'd have the hardest time recalling years from now. Simple things like the hand-washing song. Some days it seemed so important to savor them, write them down, preserve them on something solid that wouldn't get consumed in the daily grind of life. In tenth grade that same desire had led her to declare herself bound for a career in journalism. Her mom laughed, but Missy became editor of the school paper, the *Blue Ridge Chronicle*. She led the yearbook staff, and even came in second in the state forensics competition. She got voted Most Likely to Succeed in the senior superlatives election.

Shortly after placing that page in the yearbook mock-up, she'd met Paul. He'd taken her for a ride on his Harley, whipped her hair into a thousand knots, and caused this swirling tornado in her heart that had changed everything.

Jessie returned and pushed a dining room chair toward the stove, skittering it along the floor with a loud screeching sound. Across the room, Hannah jerked upright in her walker and began to cry. Missy knew she should have put her in her crib, but she was always loathe to move a sleeping child.

"Just wait," she said, putting her palm out to stop Jessica. "Let me get your sister."

Jessie continued to drag the chair toward the stove.

"Just wait, I said. It's hot, honey." Hannah began crying in earnest, holding her head at an awkward angle. "Okay, Hannah Banana, it's all right. I've got you." Missy lifted her out of the walker. "You stiff, baby? I know. Mommy should have moved you. I'm sorry. Bad Mommy." She propped Hannah on one hip, returned to the stove, and handed her a long wooden spoon. Hannah took the spoon straight to her mouth, handle end first, and began to gum it.

"Where's Daddy?" Jessica asked, climbing into the chair and cocking her head to one side like a bird.

"In the garage."

"Working on that mustache, again," said Jessie with a heavy sigh and a hand on her hip.

Missy recognized her own exasperated voice coming out of her daughter's mouth and she tried not to laugh. "It's Mustang, honey. Not mustache."

Paul had bought that shell of a Mustang, sight unseen, from a man in Kentucky, a week before the wedding and without consulting Missy. She rode with him from southwest Virginia to Northern Kentucky and back; the trip was long, hot and bumpy, but they were in love and everything was an adventure.

"Is it supposed to swerve like that?" she'd asked, craning her neck to look behind them at the red-primed hull on the fishtailing trailer he'd had to barter for at the last minute.

"Mustang's a wild horse, runs like the wind. It's got wings."

"That's Pegasus," she said. "The horse with wings."

Paul smiled. "Yeah, Pegasus. She'll fly us away." He drove with his wrist draped over the wheel. "Pegasus was gold?"

"He was white," said Missy. "Pure white. White feathers, white wings, white everything. You going to paint this car white?" She gestured toward the rear window.

"Maybe, maybe I will. Just for you, baby."

The Mustang, that rickety trailer, and an engine block purchased three days later had eaten up all of their premarriage savings, but Paul said the car was a classic and would only increase in value, so it was really an investment in their future.

"Why's he not here to help?" Jessie's indignant-child voice brought Missy back to the present. A sponge, that's what Jessie was, soaking up everything. And a nagging wifely tone was what Missy was passing along to her daughter.

"Oh, Jessie, he has to keep the Mustang running. He can't take his motorcycle everywhere. And if the Subaru breaks down we need a backup car."

If she added them up, Missy figured the hours she'd spent defending her husband, explaining away his actions, making excuses for his lack of attentiveness would now be measured in days of her life. It wasn't as if Paul was a bad man. He wasn't. He just liked to do his own thing, and he expected everyone else to like it, too. He had wanted kids as much as Missy, but once they were here, he resented the intrusion, as well as the time Missy spent attending to their needs. He wanted her to wean them before she was ready, to get babysitters early and often. He wanted them out of their bed, when it was easier for Missy to nurse at night if they were right beside her.

"Still," Jessie insisted, reaching up and pulling the spoon from Hannah's grasp, eliciting a shriek.

"Daddy loves us," Missy said. "He's just really, really busy." She took the spoon back from Jessie and handed it to Hannah, then gave Jessie a pink-handled plastic spoon. "Here," she said. "This one matches your shorts."

Jessie, still young enough to be appeased in such a manner, smiled as she stirred the pot of beans bubbling on the nearest burner.

"Careful," said Missy. "Stir slowly, or they'll pop on you."

"I know."

Missy guided Jessie's hand for several rotations then tapped the spoon on the side of the pot. "Ready to make cornbread?"

"Yum!" said Jessie, wiggling like a puppy. "Corn bed."

As Missy lifted the cast-iron skillet, a tremendous, loud, crashing sound came from the garage. The floor shook with it, and Missy stood for a moment, transfixed by morbid images. Then she rushed down the hall towards the garage door, bouncing Hannah on her hip as she ran. Hannah stared at her mother, clinging to her shirt with a tiny fist, head bobbing, spoon and other arm waving in the air.

Missy threw open the door and saw the Mustang listing off to one side, rear fender still sliding slowly down the gouged Sheetrock wall, leaving a fresh, jagged smudge.

"Paul?" she called. "Paul?" Hannah continued to stare at her, big-eyed and silent.

A wheezy groan came from the other side of the car, from where it tipped downward. She noticed Paul's steel-toed work boots sticking out towards her, jerking slightly, as if he were trying to dance while lying down.

"Oh my God." She looked around wildly. *Where to put the baby?* "Paul? Are you all right?"

Silence.

"Shit, shit, shit, shit." She opened the door to the house and slipped Hannah just inside the door, then shut it quickly. The wailing began immediately. "Just a minute, baby," she called over her shoulder as she ran to Paul. "Mommy'll be right there!"

When she rounded the front bumper, she saw his face. The rear fender of the Mustang rested just below his armpit, settling into a concave depression in his chest. He seemed to be looking at her, yet not seeing her, eyes wide and expressionless. "Shit, Paul. What do I do? Oh my God."

Paul's left arm was extended towards her feet, his fingers moved slightly, not offering any helpful direction. He couldn't talk—didn't even seem to be able to breathe. His face was reddish purple and straining, eyes bulging, like the face of a person hanging upside down.

"Don't die," she said. "Oh my God, don't die." From the other side of the door came the sounds of Hannah throwing herself bodily against it, screaming *Maaamaaa* with long wails that pulled up at the end into high-pitched shrieks. "Just a minute, Hannah," she called, looking around desperately for anything that might help. Rags, bucket, toolbox, tools.

Just under the running board she saw the orange feet of the jack stand lying on its side. She pulled it out then positioned the top of the stand under the solid part of the wheel well, beside Paul's compressed chest. The stand wouldn't lift at all, though. It only held up a car that had already been jacked.

"Don't die, Paul," she chanted. "Don't die. I'll get it off you, baby, just don't die."

She pushed with all her weight to try and shove the stand underneath, but only succeeded in making the Mustang slide farther forwards, towards the center of Paul's chest. His eyes rolled around in their sockets.

A creak sounded, as the door to the house opened and Hannah's wails increased in volume. Jessie's voice was quiet and timid, barely discernible. "Mommy? Where are you?"

"Stay inside, Jessie," Missy said, in her best drill sergeant voice, popping up just enough to look over the trunk of the car. "Take Hannah, too." Missy removed the stand and looked under the car. Just behind a cinder block, she saw the floor jack. A pan of brackish oil slid off when she jerked the cinder block towards her. It splashed onto the cement floor, rolling in shiny black lines toward the sunlight of the open garage door.

Missy moved the cinder block to one side and rolled the floor jack closer. She put it under the axle, then stood and pumped the handle. Over by the door, Jessie pulled a shrieking Hannah into the house by the collar of her onesie. The door slammed.

Paul closed his eyes.

She pumped the jack handle furiously. "No. No. No. No. No," she grunted with each push. With a creak the Mustang began to lift, easing off Paul's body slightly. She ran back around to Paul's free side and began to pull him out by his clothes. A loud ripping sound told her that his shirt had given way, but he was free.

She squeezed his cheeks and grabbed his shoulders. "Paul," she said. "Paul." She put her fingers in his hair and tugged, blew in his face, then held his nose and blew into his mouth. His lips felt dry and papery under hers and a hiss of air escaped the joining of their lips.

Paul jerked twice, then coughed and sputtered. His eyes fluttered, then opened.

"Oh, thank you, Paul. Thank you." Missy rested her head on his chest, but he winced in pain so she sat up. "Can you breathe?"

Paul nodded slightly. She smiled, then laughed with relief. "Thank God. You're okay."

He lifted his head off the cement floor then dropped it back. "My chest," he whispered.

"Okay, okay. I know. I'll drive you to Montgomery Regional. They'll check you out. Wait here. Thank God you're okay." Missy ran into the house, turned off the stove, lifted up a sobbing Hannah, pulled Jessie along by the hand, then slung her pocketbook crossways over her shoulder and lifted Jessie, too. She rushed out to the car, a child in each arm. "Daddy's hurt. He has to see the doctor. We're going now."

"Now?" asked Jessie.

"Uh-huh," said Missy, pulling the shoulder straps over Baby Hannah's head and pushing her rear back up into the car seat while she arched her back and howled.

"Hannah's sad," said Jessie.

"Uh-huh." Missy pulled the buckle across Jessie's car seat.

"She's scared bout Daddy."

"Uh-huh," said Missy. She slammed the back door, started up the Subaru and ran back to Paul.

"Come on, honey, I'll help." She placed a hand under his armpit and helped him stand then cross the yard and sit in the front seat. When she started to buckle his seatbelt he waved her off and croaked out the word, "Go."

Missy drove the back roads faster than she had ever driven before. She honked and passed recklessly. Living in a small, rural town was lovely, until you had to get to a hospital fast. The local Rescue Squad—all volunteer, and poorly funded—wasn't worth calling. The members were old as Methuselah and could barely lift a stretcher to save their own lives, let alone someone else's. Missy felt sure she could get Paul there faster—and cheaper, which heaven knows was a consideration these days. Paul had hauled only three loads last month, and none, so far, this month. As an independent trucker he couldn't haul if he didn't have the contracts, so he'd been working on the Mustang instead. But that was frustrating, too, when what little money they had got shuttled to the junkyard or the auto parts store. Missy had been stretching Hannah's diaper changes to the saggy yellow limit, trying to make them last until Paul's next paycheck, and now they had a trip to the emergency room to cover. How would they afford that?

She took a sharp curve too fast and Paul moaned and reached for the dashboard.

"Sorry," she said, but kept her speed.

"Is Daddy going to die?" Jessie asked from the backseat.

"No, honey. No," said Missy. "Daddy's going to be fine."

⌘

In the emergency room, the doctor told her how lucky she was, that Paul's blunt trauma impact was just inches from hitting the breastbone and stopping his heart. As it was, several ribs were broken, and he had a slight lung bruise, but nothing that wouldn't heal with rest.

"But the truly amazing thing," the doctor said, "is that you got the car off of him all by yourself."

"I guess so," she said. "I just did everything I could think to."

"Well, perhaps you don't know your own strength, Mrs. Connor. Stranger things have been known to happen when adrenaline is flowing."

"He really could have died?"

"From your description, I'd say he had already begun to asphyxiate."

While the doctor taped Paul's ribs, Missy took the girls to the snack machine and used the last of her change for a makeshift dinner. They returned to the waiting room and Jessie smacked loudly while eating her treats. Beside her, Missy nursed Hannah, who promptly fell asleep. Missy laid Hannah on the yellow couch, bolstered in by her purse, then stood with Jessie and rocked her body back and forth. Jessie fell asleep in the middle of chewing a gummy something; when Missy laid her on the couch, her mouth oozed a sticky purple slime. Missy lifted her head and slid one of Hannah's diapers under her cheek.

After what felt like an eternity of the same news headlines on the overhead TV, the hospital released Paul to Missy with a bottle of painkillers and the admonition to *take it easy*.

Missy stepped outside to bring the car around for Paul and the girls. The darkness of the night gave her a strange disconnected feeling since she had entered in a panic in daylight; she had no sense of how much time had elapsed. It could have been minutes. Or it could have been days and days.

The night was cool and the stars were out. Missy took a deep breath for the first time in hours and felt her chest expand with the fullness of air, then finally relax. The small hairs of her arm rose up in the night breeze, and before she realized it, she had walked past the car.

She stood at the far edge of the parking lot watching fat June bugs circle the light at the top of a tall column. She could see the uneven black horizon of the Blue Ridge Mountains against the lighter hues of the night sky. A stoplight in the distance turned from green to yellow, then to red and back again, and a pair of taillights turned a corner and disappeared. The car, the hospital, her family in the darkness behind her, all felt as if they were light-years away.

Missy took another deep, cool breath and looked straight up into the night sky. Far away the tiny white lights of an airplane moved through the stars. Her eyes tracked the movement of people flying somewhere, anywhere else, until the darkness swallowed them and she could no longer make out the lights. She turned and headed back to the car, climbed in, started the engine, and pulled around to the emergency room door.

The 30-minute drive home was filled with the soft snoring of three people asleep in the car. She admired that ability to sleep through anything. Missy used to sleep like that—not a care in the world. But that was before Paul, and before children.

In the headlights, she saw a pothole, too late to dodge it, and the passenger tire hit with a loud, tooth-rattling *whunk*; Paul squirmed and frowned, but didn't wake.

When they arrived home, it was after midnight. She carried in Baby Hannah first, her little fat cheek slack against Missy's shoulder, making a warm, wet spot of drool. Missy held her head and tipped her carefully into the crib, but she was out, arms and legs spread-eagled, lips pursed. Missy had taken the baby in first ever since her momma told her a story about a mother who left her baby in the car alone with the door open and came back out, only a few minutes later, to find a raccoon eating its brain, the baby still strapped in the car seat. That one had haunted Missy for a good long while. Her momma loved disaster stories, especially those involving maniacal killers, rabid animals, and bad mothers.

Missy carried Jessie in next, and took her to the bathroom in her sleep, or she'd pee in the bed by morning. Jessie's eyes flew open and rolled around wildly, settling on Missy and then focusing. She fixed her with a dazzling smile, said, "I love you, Mommy," in the sweetest voice, then closed her eyes, peed, kicked off her underwear and stumbled to bed without wiping.

Next Missy went to the car to help Paul, but when she got there the passenger seat was empty. She looked around and saw that he was standing by the Mustang, in the semidarkness, staring at the fender with a look of hurt and accusation.

"After all we've been through," he told it.

"Paul?"

He turned and fixed her with a wild gaze, his hair askew. "I hurt," he said.

"I know." Missy held his hand and led him away from the damage.

"You can take another painkiller," she said, and he did, then groaned as he lay back in bed. "You need an extra pillow? Anything?"

He mumbled something that Missy thought sounded like "a new life," then fell asleep.

Missy walked back out to the kitchen, which was a mess; the pot of beans still sitting on the stove, a brown skin puckering the surface of the liquid. She put on the lid and walked away. The towel, still on the floor, smelled of sour urine. Toys covered the living room floor, too, but she was exhausted. She picked up the half-chewed ear of corn from the walker and lobbed it into the trash then returned to the bedroom and crawled under the covers.

But Missy couldn't sleep. Her head roiled with strange thoughts. Beside her, Paul groaned in his sleep. She propped up on one elbow and studied his face. He was defenseless and broken, but he slept the sleep of the charmed. She mentally mapped his contours, marking the angles and lines in her brain. The doctor said the car had almost killed him—that car named after a horse that could fly them up and away from all the meanness and messiness.

She got out of bed and headed to the garage. Its wide door sat open to the night, the front end of the still-red Mustang leering upward into space where the garage door would normally descend. At the sound of her footsteps some small night creature skittered off into the darkness.

Some days Missy believed she hardly knew her husband. What did Paul want from his life? What made him feel free and alive? What were his regrets? His dreams? She didn't know. And what was worse, she didn't want to know. She should care, but she didn't.

It wasn't Paul's fault she felt trapped. Missy knew that. She married him of her own free will. She was there when the children were made. But she couldn't help feeling angry.

Angry for having given up the things that *she* wanted from life, angry for being saddled with two young children, angry for having had to lift the car—the car she never wanted to own—off his chest, the car that would have crushed his heart if she'd left it there a moment longer.

mooncalf

How you recognize a monster is dependant upon how you view normality. I have wondered if there are the makings of a monster in me. But, like Frankenstein's awkward creation, I cannot know that about myself. That will be for you to decide.

1972 is the year to go to in your mind. Picture a long and skinny baby, with a feathery bit of light brown hair, born in an old farmhouse in the backwoods Blue Ridge Mountains of Appalachia. The nearest town—a 30-minute drive over dusty gravel switchbacks and unmarked asphalt—has one unnecessary stoplight.

From birth, I grew slowly, awkwardly. I was inquisitive—alert, but mute. This surely became a disappointment to my parents, but my needs were met. Amazingly, at three years old, I began to sing. My vocal chords too spastic to master language, it was an otherworldly, wordless crooning that slid up and down the scales. My father called me his Siren, and said I sang a Siren's song. It was, he said, a special way of singing that was beautiful and haunting.

It was only later that I learned the Sirens were half-women half-birds and that they sang to men to lure them to their doom.

At four—still not using language, sidling from spot to spot in the manner of a crab—my mother carried me in public. She resisted seeing a doctor. I was simply her "late bloomer," her "petite girl," and so she hefted me, into and out of the tub, the car, my bed, for three more years, until I reached the age where others stared and frowned and then she put me down to sidle on my own. But still they stared. And still my mother resisted.

My parents subscribed to the back-to-nature movement of the seventies. Hippies, if you will, in love with love and freedom from oppression. They moved to the Blue Ridge Mountains before I was born, in the hopes of giving me a wholesome childhood, a place to grow up free from fear. My father—who had worked as a classics professor before turning to the mountains for refuge from a modern, unforgiving world—fortunately realized my intelligence and read to me. He read of great goddesses, of powerful giants and gnarled trolls. And as my attention span grew (for what else was there to entertain me, in the prison of my body, in the isolated hills?) he tutored me in tragic stories of transfiguration and loss, murder and betrayal, magic and fury.

My parents grew their own food. They put up corn, beans, and tomatoes for winter, made blackberry jam, dried apples, chopped wood, raised goats for milk and meat. For spending money and for his own use, my father grew and sold marijuana, between the rows of corn. My mother, however, preferred the mind-altering effects of LSD as her drug of choice. In fact, I believe it was acid, dropped, through the tongue of my mother and umbilically to me, that caused this shell of a body that shakes and shimmies beyond my control, that makes me the drooling, drawn-up, stuttering figure from whom others turn away.

But if you want to fully understand, you must not be afraid. You must come closer, look deeply, and imagine, for a moment, yourself as me. Imagine the pinch of ever-tightened muscles, sharp elbows that refuse to straighten, curled wrists, claws of minimal usefulness. Feel the spasm in your neck that cocks your head to the side, your facial expressions in constant flux like the sliding rainbow on an oil-slicked puddle. Feel the absence of control. And be afraid. Afraid of the dormant weakness that lies within your own body. The fragile form of you.

Or do not feel these things. But feel guilty, instead. Guilty, that in the deck of life, you got shuffled fair.

In centuries past, I would have been labeled insane. Retarded. Mooncalf. Devil child.

I would have been the otherworldly punishment for my parents' misdeeds. I would have been dropped in a river, in a bag, weighted with a rock; or suffocated, quietly, and buried behind the house; or simply refused nourishment until I starved. Malformed, I would not have been allowed to live.

Remember, though, the outward body does not betray the inner mind, and mine is whole. Its reception is superb. It is the space *between* the thought and body where impulse dies, forever wandering in corridors of lost desire. Cerebral (of or relating to the brain) palsy (uncontrollable spasm, paralysis) lets me think, hear, and string together words in my mind, but does not let me say them.

I will never know for certain if my mother's drug use caused my affliction. In any case, I believe my mother did not *mean* to harm me, any more than thalidomide mothers meant to twist and stunt their children's limbs to formless nubs. There is a certain kind of innocence, I feel, which can be ascribed to a simple *lack of intent.* This is important.

And even if my mother did make me a monstrosity, it has been her affliction, too. Having been a mother myself, I understand the complex ties of need and pain, wrought from early pleasure.

Understand this, though: forgiveness comes early when you are forced to look down daily, and forgive your arms and legs even as they disobey.

But I digress. This is not a story of forgiveness.

⌘

By the age of 18, despite my handicaps of stature and speech, I learned to walk, haltingly, the high school halls, with two four-footed canes. I often sang to myself while moving from class to class—it was a comfort and a balm. My happiest day came when I took twelve steps, individually, shakily, and crossed the riser to receive my diploma.

That fall I entered college—a small, Baptist, Virginia one, much to my atheist, liberal parents' chagrin—and there found love.

Chris was a man of God. I knew that from the start. He wanted that known, in fact, and I believed it to be true, for who else would see in me a body to love? But by *man of God*, I do not mean preacher. Rather, an honest layman, so devout and obedient, so full of self-imposed restraints that the first thing I admired about him was his will.

The first thing Chris admired about me was my singing. He said he heard me for two weeks before he finally saw me, shuffling across campus. My voice, he said, came straight from heaven and gave him shivers down his spine. Once he heard me, he had to meet me.

Chris renounced the common, earthly pleasures; I was his angel, he said, and sang with a grace that let him know he had been chosen. Chosen by God to see beauty above the physical form and thereby know divinity.

People with CP are already closer to God. They smile more. They take less for granted. They dream at night of walking and talking, unimpeded, then wake, happy to have experienced it, even in a dream. And I can tell you that a person wears a soul like an extra, shadowy skin. So don't feel sorry for me. I have much. And I have Chris.

At college, Chris walked beside my motorized cart, escorting me to classes. He met me at the end of the day and accompanied me to my specially equipped dorm. He talked to me for hours, laying out his plans for life, content to have only my smile as response. He begged me to sing to him and when I did he would lay his head upon my lap, closing his eyes, smiling in pleasure. Chris loved me, in spite of, and because of, my disability. I couldn't believe my own good fortune.

"College girls are so impure," he said to me, after a month of our near inseparability. "You are full of goodness, though. My saving grace."

That was the night he finally kissed me.

"M-i-i-ne," I answered, pushing out the word, feeling it first, willing it up. I smiled with what Chris called my wide-open love grin, all teeth and happy gums, to let him know he meant the same to me. I'm certain he understood. He lifted the edge of the flowered scarf around my neck, wiped my lower lip, and kissed me.

I grew wings with that kiss—lifted up—like lily white Pegasus, born of a Gorgon's ugly blood.

"Will you be my helpmeet?" he asked.

I loved his formal, old-fashioned words, and I over-nodded in response, the way I do when too excited. With his hands he held my head to stop me, then laughed and told me I was beautiful.

Shortly thereafter, Chris took me home to meet his pious parents, and they were kind, if a little strained, when asking questions that I took too long, and too few words, to answer; or when I nodded and smiled to Chris, asking him, with a look, to answer for me. They sat with hard smiles, and patient faces. They nodded, betraying only with their shifting feet how much they longed to see Chris walk away.

Chris took me to his church. The hushed atmosphere of restraint and expectation spoke to my soul. It was a balm, truly, for having grown up in an environment of liberal freedom and excess, exposed to antireligious cynicism, and daily drug use, I longed to experience the other side. For me, the other, forbidden side, meant piety, humility, and the joy of long-suffering. I had to be good, just that way, in order to rebel.

Chris and I were married—after I was saved and baptized, of course—and I left college to be at his side. He became a church counselor, in nearby Bristol, for troubled teens. He spoke out against abortion and cited our life together as an example of what any child could become. We dreamed of starting a family of our own.

Learning the act of physical love was a delight, and had seemed, for all my life, something I would forever be denied. But I always had urges. Maybe more than most, trapped as I am, in this unattractive, uncooperative shell. Chris was patient, and the joy in his face when we loved, his abandon and surrender, transported me and gave me strength. Afterwards, my spasms would lessen for hours.

In our early marriage, I spent my days struggling to fix Chris's nightly meal. The frustrating hours became my labor of love for him—my gratitude for his love of me. I learned how best to move the pots around, and what dishes not to cook—hot sauces, for instance, and recipes that required chopping. Chris was patient with me, and almost never fussed. I knew it was a measure of his love.

Within two months of our vows, I became pregnant. This was a worry, and a delight, as I imagine it is for most women. Chris grew even more loving and attentive, and the first six months were easy, with no noticeable sickness, and only minor discomfort. My walking canes became more difficult to balance as the gravitational center of my body changed; the spasms more troubling as I worried that the baby could be affected. I became especially anxious when I felt a frequent, regular, jerking coming from within. I sang to the baby inside me, but nothing I could do would make it stop. I met Chris at the door, worry on my face, and put his hand to my belly. He called his mother. She said it was the baby's hiccups.

By the seventh month, I was no longer visiting, writing, or calling my own parents. This was troubling, but after one particularly disagreeable visit Chris and I agreed that their influence would not have been a good one for the baby. I missed my mother, but also didn't, for I loved Chris so. I also knew she didn't understand my newfound righteousness, and it was a relief not to have to explain.

I was also, perhaps naturally, more worried than most new mothers, both because of my disability, and because we had chosen to give birth at home without medical intervention. We trusted, instead, that the Lord would let nothing happen to our child or to me.

Jonah's birth was painful, but Chris's loving support helped me to endure it. His name began as a joke, with Chris referring to the child inside of me as "Jonah" since, he said, it was living in the belly of a whale, ha-ha. But the prebirth nickname stuck, and when the child proved to be a boy, it followed naturally.

For the first few weeks, I was able to do little more than nurse Jonah and attend to him, as he was a needy child, frequently wailing and red-faced, and seeming, like God's own Jonah, to be angry unto death. I would have preferred a happier baby, and on occasion—as I imagine all new mothers must, my own especially— I questioned why God had chosen to give me such a difficult child instead.

To carry Jonah, I fashioned a makeshift sling from a bedsheet. By first moving it under him, then leaning over and slipping my head and arm through the narrowest part, I could in this way lift him and move him from room to room. The creak of the crutches and the jerk and swing of my hips comforted him, as he had heard and felt them long before he was born.

It was when I was dressing him, one day, that my feelings of motherly ambivalence changed. While pulling the tiny shirt over his one-month-old head, it stuck halfway down. The constriction panicked him and his shriek was high and thin. When I finally got the neck of the shirt down, his eyes were wide. He looked imploringly at me, and seemed so helpless, suddenly, which of course he had been all along, but it was as if I was only just seeing it. I put my face near his belly, blew softly and made cooing noises. He calmed, his eyes relaxed, and he laughed. Just a silly jerking gurgle, but it was enough to make me fall in love. In love with my beautiful, beautiful baby boy.

Even so, Jonah remained difficult to calm. Chris helped when he was able, and his church was flexible at first, but the church was also growing, and with that growth came more calls in the middle of the night, more adolescent angst acted out into our lives. It was a strain on us both, and, I feared, our marriage.

"Please don't misunderstand," said Chris. "I know he is a precious gift. And that we need to nurture him in the ways of Lord. I want to be the best earthly father I can be. But some days I wish it was just you and me, like it used to be."

I looked at Chris, not sure what to say, or what I could say to let him know I understood. I nodded and he continued.

"He's just so loud. He cries like his lungs are on fire. I come home from work and the house smells like dirty diapers, and you're always so tired. Our bed stinks of sour milk and there's white drips down the bed frame. I wanted Jonah, but I thought it would be easier or something. Why'd God give us this suffering child? What'd we do? Jonah's so hard when he cries. I want to help, but I don't know what he wants."

His voice trailed off, and I nodded again.

From the bedroom Jonah's wail rose slowly and spread into the room. Chris flinched at the sound, and pulled away from me. I felt the weight so heavy on him. I would have done anything to see Chris happy.

By two months of age, Jonah's lungs were well developed. He had a wisp of Chris's red hair above each tiny ear, and a pink face, but none of Chris's freckles. Maybe babies grow into them. I don't know. But I do know that I began to notice Jonah eating less and fussing even more.

My mother-in-law pronounced him "colicky" but no one told me what that meant, and it seemed a neutral way to say that Jonah had a crabby disposition. I sang to him, which sometimes helped. But Chris stayed away more, arriving later in the evenings, claiming work; I knew it was the baby's cries that drove him from our home.

The night of Jonah's worst crying, neither one of us could stand the noise. At two a.m. Chris turned to me in bed. "It's an hour, now, he's been crying."

I nodded.

"I've got work in the morning. It's two a.m. I can't take this."

I hated to see Chris so upset. I made a sympathetic noise in my throat and nodded again.

"What can I do? I don't know what to do."

"Wa-a-a-lk," I said, smiling encouragement. He got up from the bed and left the room without answering.

I lay there and listened to them pace the floor as Jonah shrieked, punctuated with Chris's own desperate cries of, "What? What?"

and "Stop crying!" Jonah would quiet slightly with each of Chris's outbursts and I could picture him, eyes wide and afraid, face to face in reckoning with his angry father.

The sonorous wailing approached and receded as Chris circled through the house, down the long hall, into the living room, and back. Occasionally the sound of Jonah's crying would stutter and I knew Chris was patting his back as firmly as he dared.

Chris entered the room then, with Jonah at his shoulder, arms straight out, pushing away, screaming baby bloody murder. "I don't know what to do anymore. Try to feed him," he said, leaning over and opening his hands dropping Jonah the last inch onto the bed. Jonah's breath caught for a moment and the crying stopped abruptly. I bared my breast and turned him towards me. Chris stood and watched in the half-light from the hallway door. Jonah latched on, sucked for a second, then turned his head away and cried.

I shrugged and smiled up at Chris.

"Will you quit smiling?" Chris said over Jonah's mewling. "It's not funny." His face was hard. I smiled wider, but tears began to slip from my eyes.

"Wha-a-at?" he said, drawing the word out as I might have. Then, "Don't do that," in a gentler tone. I tasted salty wetness in the corners of my stupidly smiling mouth. "I'm sorry," Chris said. "I know you can't control it. I know that. It just set me off. It's okay."

I nodded. "Ba-a-a-th?" I said.

Chris looked at me as he pulled at the wet and rumpled shoulder of his pajama top. "Good idea," he said. He lifted the baby and I gathered my canes and followed them to the bathroom, hobbling down the hall in the wake of Jonah's wails.

By the time I got there, Chris had the water on, and had set Jonah on the plush rug of the bathroom floor, still crying and flailing his arms in the air. I sat down outside the door and took my clothes off, then held my arms out to Chris. He stepped over the baby, gathered me up and placed me in the warm water. I leaned against the plastic inflatable pillow and Chris placed Jonah on my legs. I wetted the washcloth from the side of the tub, and let warm water trickle over Jonah's tiny belly and legs. I wiped his face gently. His body rocked with the sloshing of the water.

Chris leaned forward and turned off the tap. "Call me when you're ready to get out." He laid a folded towel on the floor beside the tub.

"Ka-a-ay." My face drew into a smile and I nodded.

As the water dribbled over Jonah, his eyes closed and his cries slipped into longer and lower tones, drawing out in songlike vowels so that I knew he was quieting finally, singing himself to sleep as he sometimes did after a long spell of crying.

I laid the warm washcloth over his tummy, turned him slightly, and offered my breast. In this relaxed state, he drank fully.

I nodded off as I sat there in the warm water, nursing my child. With a start, I caught myself and jerked awake. The water was cooling and Jonah was sound asleep, breathing deeply.

"Chri-i-is," I called from the tub. I waited. No answer. "Chri-i-is," I tried again, more loudly. Still, there was no response. I am not able to yell as most people can, and I assumed Chris was asleep, tired after so much time pacing the floors. I wasn't sure what to do. Jonah would be cold soon, and needed covering. We couldn't stay in the tub all night.

I called Chris two more times, but it was clear he wasn't coming. Since my left arm has less spasticity, I leaned well forward and slid Jonah into the crook of it. I then lifted that arm and set it on the edge of the tub with the washcloth under it. Jonah stirred, but continued to sleep. I turned my body and got on my knees as best I could, then slowly slid my arm down, until the edge of the tub was under my armpit, and my forearm and Jonah were tipping within inches of the folded towel. With my feet I pushed off against the far side of the tub and fell forwards, just managing to slither sideways and avoid Jonah.

After righting myself, I pulled down the hand towel and placed it over Jonah, then retrieved my nightgown and dressed myself. Scooting and squeaking my bare legs along the hardwood floor, I slid Jonah down the hall on his towel, diapered him with difficulty, located the sling, and managed to return him to the crib still asleep.

I gathered my canes, then creaked and clonked my way back to bed. Chris slept through it all, and as I lay beside him in the dim light, I admired the angelic curve of his sweetly sleeping face.

At 4:30 a.m., I awoke to Jonah sobbing in earnest again, full out, lungs bellowing, in a way I hadn't even known a baby could cry. It hurt just to listen to it, and although I felt I should go to him, and soothe him, I was exhausted from my middle-of-the-night bathtub wrestling. So I nudged Chris awake, instead.

"Huh?" he said, sitting up with a start. "Wha?"

I pointed towards the nursery and let Jonah's cries answer for me.

"Okay, okay." Chris pushed up from the bed and with hunched shoulders, started down the hall. I could hear him talking to Jonah as he entered the nursery. "What?" he said. "What is it?" The squeals of a rubber squeaky toy being rapidly squeezed. The rattle of the side of the crib going down. A heavy sigh. "Need your momma?"

Chris returned, I tried to nurse, nothing worked. Physically my body couldn't handle much more stress, and my spasms were increasing. I tried to say "tired" and it came out more like, "ti-i-i-ie." But Chris knew.

"Of course you're tired," he said. "I'm tired, too. Exhausted. How am I supposed to walk the floor all night with a screaming baby, then work all day?"

"Ba-a-a-ack?" I said, hoping that would help. But I felt my mouth pull into a nervous smile, and I turned my face away.

"Back? Putting him back is your solution? He doesn't sleep any better there, he doesn't cry any less. I can't sleep with the crying either. I might as well be walking." He left the room again and I followed the sound of his footsteps mixed with Jonah's howls, which by now had a gravelly edge of hoarseness to them. Did babies get laryngitis? I had the perverse thought, then, that if he would only scream himself voiceless, there would be no more problem.

I didn't know what Chris thought as he paced the floors. I only knew he was a saint to be the father that Jonah needed, that I needed. I dozed off feeling blessed.

I awakened, suddenly, to the sound of Chris speaking again. His cadence and tone were strange. His voice was breathy and frantic, and held an edge of panic. "Stop-stop-stop-stop-stop-stop!" he said.

Jonah's cries stilled and I heard the side of the crib going back up. Chris returned to bed, breathing heavily, and fell asleep.

I lay there listening hard in the stillness and staring at the blackness of the ceiling. An uneasy feeling curled itself around my insides and tightened. Not wanting to make any noise, I slid out of bed to the floor. I crawled and sidled crablike down the hall towards the baby's room.

From my position on the floor, the hall stretched and lengthened in the manner of a dream, until it seemed the baby's room was so very far away, as if I'd never make it.

I was out of breath by the time I reached the doorway to Jonah's nursery. I crossed the floor to his crib and pulled myself up on the side of it. Jonah was breathing quietly, and a little roughly, the residuals of his extended cry—the snubs, as we called them. But I watched his face and saw that he was peaceful. Relief flooded through me. I returned to bed.

In the morning, as he always did, Chris brought Jonah to our bed before he left for work, so that I could nurse and attend to him easily. He laid Jonah gently down and kissed him on the head. "Bye-bye, babies," he said to us, his daily parting phrase. "See you in the afternoon." Jonah slept, quiet after his night of fussing. He had no interest in eating, so I let him lie beside me in the bed and stroked the soft skin of his bare legs. It was moments like these when the pure love of motherhood welled up inside me, full to bursting. It was like getting the chance to know my Chris from his babyhood. What a gift.

Within a few hours, though, I began to be concerned. My breasts were full, and I knew Jonah should be nursing. He was sleeping soundly, though, and when I lifted and dropped his arm, it hit the bed like a rag doll's. I rocked his shoulders slightly, but still he slept. I put a dripping breast to his slack lips, hoping to convince him to nurse, as he would sometimes do, even when not fully awake. He did not stir.

I raised an eyelid. His big black pupil stared out at me, an unseeing hole. I raised the other. In one corner, a small spot of red bloomed like a rose. His face was slack and peaceful.

I called Chris at work, but I was agitated, and couldn't form the words.

"I don't understand," Chris said. "Calm down."

I tried again to speak.

"Is it the baby?"

"Ye-e-es."

"I don't hear him crying. Is he crying?"

"No-o-o."

"Well is he awake?"

"No-o-o."

"You mean he's sleeping?"

"Ye-e-es."

"Give me a minute here. I've got to think." Silence. "You're calling me because you think he's sleeping too much?"

"Ye-e-es!"

"Well, for heaven's sake. Let him sleep, honey. Enjoy the break. You worry too much. Sleep can't hurt him. Haven't you ever heard, 'Let sleeping babies lie'?" He chuckled. "It'll be okay. Really. I promise."

Okay is a relative term.

Did Jonah cry anymore?

No. He did not. I let him sleep. I lay beside him and touched his body and felt his tiny breaths upon my hand. He lay a few more hours there with me, then left, quietly. There was no need to call anyone.

I lay there instead, next to my beautiful baby. I sang to him and thought of all his nevers. Never would he take a first step, lose a tooth, start school. Never would he feel the crack of a softball against the bat. Never would he know the joy of a puppy. Never would he have a first date or first kiss. Never would he hold his own child in his arms. Never would he know how much I loved him. Never would he grow into his freckles.

thunderstones

Olivia never should have started dating a geologist. That's clear as quartz as she stands in the Museum of Natural History, Rob looking over her shoulder, his hot geologist's breath tickling her ear, her pulse pounding in her temples. Whoever heard of spending hours looking at rocks? And that's what they are, really, just big, lumpy Swiss cheese rocks. Rocks that look like steel or iron when you cut them in half, and rocks that have come a long way for sure, but rocks just the same.

Rob is breathing over her shoulder because she's found the only interesting thing in the whole museum. Unless of course you count the Hope diamond, which God knows *she* hasn't seen, since the gunmetal gray rocks are too riveting to forsake, especially for a bunch of silly, sparkling, jelly-colored gems.

Olivia touches her finger to the freestanding computer screen that lets you design your own meteorite and crash it to earth. She picks the smallest, baseball-sized one, and brings it into Kansas farmland at night. When she touches "launch" the bumpy meteorite hurtles toward her through black space like a Star Trek asteroid, then point of view changes, and she's looking down from above, watching it crash to earth.

"Cool beans," Rob says in an awed half-whisper.

Rob has a runner's body, ropey and thin, and when he holds

Olivia, the top of her head fits right under his chin. He has thick, wavy hair, the color of pebbled sand and loves old Bob Dylan songs, the ones like poems put to music. He sings along, never missing a word. In his dorm he's started a *Jeopardy!* craze. She could just eat him up when he commandeers the lounge and calls out the questions to the answers before anyone else. *What is Cadmium, Alex?*

Olivia's parents love Rob, too. Every time she comes home from Emory and Henry College they ask her if she's gotten a ring yet. They'll be happy as a bug when she shows them what Rob gave her last night in the Crystal City Marriot: his grandmother's diamond. Olivia wrapped toilet tissue around the underside of the ring this morning in the hotel in order to make it stay on her finger. Rob's grandmother was a big woman.

After Rob's roommate dropped out last semester, they had the whole suite to themselves. He could totally get her juices going, too, all squirmy and squishy in the heated air of his upper bunk. Hours would pass in igneous bliss. Whew. Just thinking about it makes her want to suck his breath into her mouth right there in the Geology, Gems and Minerals exhibit. But when she turns her body toward him, Rob leans past her to take his turn at the make-your-own-meteorite screen. With his shoulders hunched and his eyes stuck on the screen Rob picks a massive meteorite and sends it, super fast, into a bustling metropolis. Devastation explodes across the screen.

Olivia's fingertips tingle. Her feet sweat inside her shoes like the steaming sauna rocks in the ritzy Richmond Carlton. First Rob explained how porous lava rocks retain heat and moisture making them the perfect sauna stones, then they locked the door, draped a towel over the window and did it right there on the redwood slats while hot air seared her lungs and sweat dripped into her ears.

Olivia's parents would die if they knew she and Rob were staying in a hotel together. They would die, and then they would kill her. She and Rob are supposed to be staying with his relatives but she knows her mom would never call to check.

Fortunately, Rob's parents are loaded. They live in Lynchburg, and trust him to spend his graduation money righteously even if he is a geologist and talks about the world being billions of years old, which they don't believe for a minute. Rob's dad is a bigwig in the fundamentalist church, which scares Olivia, although she's never said so. She grew up lapsed Methodist and all she remembers of church are the rituals. Knowing such things as when to stand, and when to sit, and what to say and sing, makes all the difference to Olivia. It makes her feel like she belongs.

In the beginning, Olivia fended off Rob's advances. She meant to save herself for marriage—she really did. But each time he stopped, she chafed with want for the slippery moistness of Rob's lips against her skin, thirsted as if she lay cracked and dry in the desert instead of sliding in the slow press of his body against hers, breathing his very air into her lungs like life.

Olivia finds a continuous film about a giant meteorite that struck earth 65 million years ago. Computer graphics recreate the impact. It hits just below Florida and makes a huge tidal wave that crashes all the way past the Great Lakes, scouring the land bare as it sweeps back into the sea. Wildfires spontaneously ignite, creating giant smoke clouds that block sunlight for a year. Seventy percent of all species are eliminated. The rats and shrews survive. They thrive. From this came humans.

She turns away. Olivia can't bear total destruction, even from a distance of 65 million years. Did those wicked things still hit earth? She doesn't know what she would do if she had to always worry about things falling out of the sky. Live a helpless, waiting life? Horrible.

She really should sit down. There's a bench beside a huge chunk of meteorite that has a little sign saying *Please Touch* but Olivia doesn't dare. It might sizzle, or steam, or sting. She couldn't take that.

Across from her is a television screen showing four amateur videos of a meteorite that hit Westchester, New York in 1992. It landed on the trunk of a woman's car. There's a full-color photo of her blackened, misshapen Chevy Malibu. What did she tell her insurance company? Does a meteorite fall under *acts of God*?

Rob wanders in front of the display case and blocks her view. "Hey, Liv," he says after a moment's pause, "did you read about this one?" He shifts his backpack higher on his shoulder and turns to look at her. "It says here that it came through these people's roof while they were watching TV, and bounced into the living room and landed under a table. Can you imagine?"

But she *can* imagine. That's the whole problem. She can feel the shudder of the heavy metal space rock slamming into the roof, hear the screech of shingle and Sheetrock giving way as it rips through the ceiling, and smell the smoke as that tiny piece of Mars lies smoldering at her feet. She looks up at Rob and opens her mouth to say this but all that comes out is a little puff of air.

"You feel okay?" He grabs her hands and pulls her to her feet. When she looks up at him, he kisses her and says, "My feet hurt. Let's go in here. Watch a movie." He leads her into the quiet theater area and she relaxes into the padded seat. Olivia is tired. They left school over a week ago and in that time they've seen three battlefields, four James River plantations, Luray Caverns, Natural Bridge, Yorktown, Jamestown, Colonial Williamsburg, Richmond, and now Washington, D.C.

The movie starts. It's *The Tumultuous History of the Solar System*, and she's getting absolutely breathless listening to the voiceover describe this cranky crust of earth on which she so precariously sits. On screen there's a molten hose of orange lava spewing out from the coast of Hawaii followed by footage of a fiery white comet shooting sparks across the night sky. The deep-voiced announcer declares, "Our earth is constantly dying and being reborn, and parts of this land are only minutes old."

Olivia didn't need to know that. She staggers out of the theater as the film restarts to a new crop of hapless viewers, then slides down the wall and sits outside the exit. The wall across from her is a huge aerial map of the Appalachian Mountains. The placard says they were formed 530 million years ago, when Africa slammed into North America and all those sediments that had been layering down for millions of years got pushed into the air, crumpling like car hoods in a head-on collision.

⌘

Olivia stares into the distant blue haze of those crumpled-car-hood-mountains the very next day when they drive to Lynchburg to tell Rob's parents the news.

"Really, Liv, don't worry." Rob turns onto the last street before his parents' driveway. "They'll love you. You're great. What's not to love?"

"Plenty." She pulls off the oversized ring with its toilet tissue padding and slips it into her pocket.

"We'll have it sized," Rob says and pats her arm. Olivia thinks of the cutting and soldering, the removal of a bead of gold and the permanent change to fit her finger, forever and ever, till death do us part and her lungs constrict with a fiery pain.

"Did you tell them we've been traveling together?"

"God, no," says Rob. "Don't say anything, either. Dad would have a cow, and Mom'd go to bed for a week. This is an overnight visit to meet them. That's all."

They pull into the long driveway. It's a huge southern mansion two-story deal with four white columns. A silver-haired couple emerges from the front door and strides toward the car like they've rehearsed.

"And you must be Olivia," says the woman with her arms outstretched. She's trim and pretty and Olivia accepts the stiff, upper-body-only hug. There's an awkward moment during which neither woman knows where to turn her head.

For dinner they have a roast with miniature whole vegetables perched in gravy. Effie the cook brings it to the table on an oval platter before she leaves for the day. The perfect little pearl onions, new potatoes, baby carrots, and embryonic squash surround the big hunk of meat, glistening in presentation.

At age five, Olivia pulled up and ate two full sweet rows of immature carrots in her grandmother's vegetable garden. For her heady snack she was soundly spanked, her fists still clutching the feathery green foliage. Her grandmother said you had to let things grow. Enjoy them in their fullness, warts and all.

"So," Rob's father says, "what do you study in school, Olivia?"

She wipes her hands on the linen napkin. "I haven't really decided yet."

"Mmmm."

"I mean, I don't have to declare a major until fall. But, I like psychology, I guess. And art."

"Oh, you could do art therapy with mental patients," says Rob's mother with a bright smile.

"Gloria gets these grand ideas," says Rob's father.

"Oh, you." Gloria swishes her hand in his direction. "Don't listen to him, Olivia."

"So you would be a psychiatrist?" his father asks.

"Well I'm deciding still, trying lots of things, actually kind of hoping a major will pop up and declare me, I guess." She wipes her mouth and smiles.

"Yes, well. A career isn't always necessary."

"Actually, Mom, Dad," says Rob, and Olivia thinks *No! Don't.* "We've decided to get married."

Gloria finishes chewing and swallows quickly. "Married?" she says, then adds, "How wonderful." She holds her glass out towards her husband. "Isn't that wonderful, Mark?"

"Quite."

"Olivia has Gram's ring," says Rob.

"Does she?" Mark speaks into the rim of his glass.

"It's very pretty," says Olivia.

"Married," says Gloria, pushing a miniature squash along the edge of her gold-rimmed china.

"You're the first to know," says Olivia. "I haven't even told my mother yet."

"How sweet." Gloria's voice is lilting. "Isn't that sweet, Mark?"

"Very."

"Oh, we have so much to plan," says Gloria.

"Like what church to get married in," says Mark.

"Dad," says Rob.

"Church?" Olivia looks from Rob to his father.

"Can we do this later?" asks Rob.

"For the wedding," Mark says, ignoring his son. "Where *do* you go to church, Olivia?"

"I don't think—"

"Nonsense, Robbie," says his mother. "Olivia doesn't mind. Do you, dear?"

Rob gives Olivia a look she doesn't understand. "Um, no. No, of course not. I mean, my mom was—is—Methodist. And my dad, well, he doesn't go much. But Emory and Henry is a Methodist school so I get that there."

"Methodist, of course. We learned about E&H when Rob transferred there from Liberty University."

"I'm really glad he did." Olivia nudges Rob's foot under the table.

"Well, they don't exactly study how the earth was formed at Liberty," says Rob with a chuckle.

"Don't they?" Mark raises an eyebrow, his fork poised in midair.

"Okay, well, six days doesn't give a geologist much to go on."

"I thought we were talking about your wedding," says Gloria. "I want to talk about that. *Have* you picked a church?"

Rob takes his napkin from his lap, rests both elbows on the table and leans toward his mother. "We haven't really discussed *where*, Mom."

"Okay, then, a summer wedding at least?" Gloria looks from face to face.

"Look, we don't know that either. Maybe not till I finish graduate school. The UVA geology program is really tough."

"Geology."

"Yes, Dad." Rob pushes back from the table. "You know what I study. Don't—"

"Nonsense, dear," says Gloria. "Sit down. Let your father talk." She turns to Olivia. "You like all that geology stuff?"

Olivia looks around the table. "Well, I like Rob, and it's what he does."

"Of course," says Gloria. "You have a dress picked out?"

"A dress?" Olivia pictures herself facedown in the roast. *Breathe slowly,* she tells herself, *just breathe slowly.*

"You know, my old wedding dress would look darling on you. It's lovely, all-white, just precious."

White. Precious.

"Back to the church," says Mark. "Our religion is the cornerstone of our lives, Olivia. And Rob is our only child. We want to do this right, and we'd like to welcome his future wife as a member of the family. I'd like to know: what does the Methodist church teach?"

"Teach?"

"Yes. About baptism, for instance."

"Baptism?" Olivia says.

"Full-immersion? Or sprinkling of drops?"

"Well," she says, taking a deep breath and rearranging her silver steak knife, "I was baptized as a baby, so I don't remember it, but my mom had me christened and I have godparents and all."

"You don't remember being baptized?"

"Um, no. I was six weeks old, so I don't." She smiles. "But I'm guessing God does."

"Olivia, God wants us to come to Him through His son," says Mark. "He wants us to *ask* for our salvation. What good is being washed in the blood of the Lamb if we're too small to know what it means?"

"Well, it's still a baptism." Olivia chokes slightly on the slippery roundness of a pearl onion.

"Oh, our church had the most wonderful Revival last week," says Gloria. "Six people accepted the Lord as their personal savior and were baptized right then. It was beautiful."

Rob takes a big breath to say something but his mother chimes in again. "I've got a lovely idea." She claps her hands. "Why don't we all go to church together? Tomorrow. You can leave from there to take Olivia home."

"Excellent idea," says Rob's father.

"You'll love our church," she says to Olivia. "Won't she Robbie?"

Olivia looks to Rob. He shrugs. "All right," he says.

They sleep in separate rooms that night, of course. Olivia gets Rob's old yellow-walled, green-shag-carpeted room. An early rock collection lines his childhood desk in dusty rows, from amethyst to zircon in separate small square boxes. She falls asleep to the odor of alphabetized ores and labeled minerals.

In the dark hours of the night one side of the bed presses down and Rob is there, whispering *Baby*, sliding his hot hands under her nightgown, breathing into her hair.

"Your parents."

"Quietly," he says, his urgent breath against her ear. Her belly seizes, pulling towards his sudden weight and warmth above her in the dark.

"We can't. What if they hear?"

"Shhh," Rob says, a wordless rising hiss that lifts her body up to his. Olivia craves this urgency, this magic weightless drop into surrender, this ownership, this thing that they will always have between them, this thing that binds her to him.

"Oh my god," she whispers, clutching his back in the heavy darkness, pulling him to her. She is dying, giving over, opening, body and soul. Her sigh fills the room, swelling the air with a heady, fervent hush.

⌘

Over breakfast at the Cracker Barrel she watches Rob's parents for signs that they heard the bed frame thumping the wall. When the food arrives, she digs in, happy and starved, but Mark clears his throat and everyone looks at her, waiting. She puts down her fork and they say grace over the pancakes while her heart hammers away in the cave of her ribs; she places a hand above her breast to calm it.

At church they sit three rows from the front. Rob stretches his arm across the back of the pew and cups Olivia's shoulder. She expects the lights to dim but they don't and the preacher strides out in a jaunty suit. He makes jokes; the congregation laughs.

She eyes Rob sideways. Last night she had been breathless with the glorious thrill of surrender, of opening a door to her passionate self, a door that terrified her if she thought too much about it— that closed off the hungry monsters that appalled her in the sober light of day. Who was that moaning, writhing woman of the night before? That woman who clutched and convulsed, who would have gladly chosen death over chastity?

This morning, Rob's manner is pious and solicitous in a way that confuses Olivia. He's smiling and nodding, chuckling at the preacher's jokes. Two seats over, Mark holds his bible and leans forward to utter the occasional, encouraging, "Amen." Gloria, three seats away, is eclipsed by Mark, but Olivia can hear her light giggle and sighs of approval. She can feel her future mother-in-law's insipid happiness creeping toward her through the pew cushions.

During the sermon, which is about submitting your will to God's, the preacher paces back and forth, treading the front of the church like a stage. "No one here today," he says, "is here by accident." He runs a hand through his thick black hair. "God has brought you here for a reason." He looks smack at Olivia and a tiny shiver climbs the ladder of her spine.

"God is trying hard to reach you, my friend. All *you* have to do is answer." He strides away from the pulpit and stops. Olivia's fingers burn under the nails. She looks down expecting to see them glow. She stares until she's dizzy but they're just her normal hands.

"We don't know when the Lord will come to take us. It could happen today. You could walk right out that door and be hit by a bus, or a big old rock, straight from outer space. When God wants you, He takes you, my friend. Will you be ready?" Olivia watches his lips move and purse, his teeth come together and smile. She can feel his voice move throughout her body.

In the front row, a woman with dark hair and gray roots lifts her hands above her shoulders, palms up, and sways from side to side. Rob squeezes Olivia's shoulder and pulls her close. She can't take a full breath—it's as if iron bands are encircling her chest. In that colonial cooper's shop, the man in breeches and buckled shoes hammered the last hoop down around the staves and crushed them up against each other, tight as a drum, bound them together till even water couldn't get between them.

"Let me ask you now," the preacher says, "do you really want to leave here today without the assurance of everlasting life?" His voice falters and his face crumples. Olivia's own throat constricts in sympathy. "You can have it my friend." He speaks in a near whisper. "All you have to do is open the door."

"A-men," rumbles the congregation.

Organ music starts and everyone stands. Olivia grips the pew-back in front of her for support. The preacher slides his silky words between the lines of the hymn.

"With every head bowed and every eye closed."

Softly and tenderly Jesus is calling...

"I want you to search your heart."

Calling for you and for me...

"Search your heart to see if there's room in there for God."

See, on the portals He's waiting and watching...

"He has room for you."

Watching for you and for me.

"Do you have room for Him?"

Even with her eyes closed she feels the room spinning. God wants her. She sways slightly. He *wants* her. Her hands are on fire. He wants *her*.

The air swells with the weight of the entire congregation, singing and waiting and praying just for her. Her knees are weak as water. Her eyes burn. Her head will surely burst into flame. Images of the trip run through her mind: early morning mist hanging over a deserted battlefield like long forgotten smoke; a bent, old cooper pounding his barrels into rightness and rectitude; her boyfriend dripping down on her in the cloistered heat of the sauna; a fiery spurt of lava hissing its way into the cool, blue ocean; a hurtling meteorite headed right for her.

All she has to do is give in.

multicolored tunneled life

For Lois Gibbs, Love Canal survivor and activist

S ylvie weighs a warm river stone in the palm of each hand like a balance, deciding which to keep and which to toss. She looks up as Hank casts a long fly that drops weightless into a silver pool; water swirls and eddies all around him.

Hank loves to fish.

Sylvie loves to set her rhythms to the warble of the water's ceaseless song. She loves the inevitable search for the perfect marbled river rock to cup its sacred smoothness and nestle the shape of eons in her hand.

Sylvie sits up and waves to Hank, then scoots her rear from side to side, scrunching the pebbles at the water's edge into a customized seat. She closes her eyes and leans back against a boulder, tilting her face towards a shaft of sunlight that burns pink through her eyelids and falls full and warm upon her forehead, cheeks, and neck. She concentrates on the music of the river: the mellow, liquid plink-plunks of water flowing over rocks, the nasal whine of late summer cicadas, and the background harmony of a wood thrush's lonely call, *ee-o-lay*.

This is their eighth summer returning to the river, and Sylvie never tires of it. Little River reminds her of the rivers of her childhood and although it's aptly named—especially for this end of the county—it has a presence nonetheless, and like Hank, has more than held her interest through the years.

This has been the driest summer in her memory, though, and the river is down at least three feet from last year. It feels diminished—dirtier, and rockier—and Hank has fewer pools in which to fish but lots of rocks to walk upon, which he does, since he opted not to bring his waders today.

She hears a shout of triumph and opens her eyes to see Hank about 300 yards down the riverbed with a thrashing fish at the end of his line. Even from this distance she sees that he's smiling. She places the shapelier of the two stones in her pocket and begins stepping rock to rock to join him in his victory.

Sylvie loves her husband, has loved him ever since she met him. Mister Popular, athletic, sandy-haired, happy-go-lucky Hank—Big Man On Campus, as the brothers of Psi Epsilon used to say. Hank was captain of the soccer team at UVA, back when soccer was barely heard of in the southern states, and Pele was at the height of popularity in South America. Sylvie and Hank met at a game actually, his senior year at UVA, her junior year at Virginia Tech, arch rivals, *culture vs. agriculture* he used to tease. They could hardly wait to get married and start a family.

By the time Sylvie makes it across the slippery rocks to Hank he already has the fish on a stringer and back in the water, where it flails about in frustration. "Be right back," he says. "Saw another jump down river."

Sylvie squats to watch the captive fish. It alternately rests and curves its body in an attempt to rid itself of the metal rod running down its mouth and out past the gill. With a sudden sinking urge, Sylvie wants to set it free. She can picture the grateful swish of its tail as the fish takes a giant pain-free breath and escapes, weary, but wiser. The fish turns its eye upward to study Sylvie and she feels its wordless pleading. She's got to help it. She'll figure out what to tell Hank later. The fish can't wait. It's dying before her eyes. She squats lower on her haunches and reaches down into the water with both hands, circling them around the fish's slender body.

The fish flips as if to chase its tail and a dorsal spine catches in her thumb. She cries out and jumps back in surprise nearly upsetting her precarious perch on the rock.

"What? What is it?" Hank says from behind her. "You okay?"

"Fine," Sylvie says past the thumb in her mouth. "I'm fine. I thought you were downstream?"

"I was. Damn fish took my lucky fly."

"Oh." She points at the remaining fish. "This one's dying, Hank. Look."

"Dying?" he says. "Poor thing." Sylvie isn't sure if he's mocking her. She decides to think the best of Hank and smiles. She's learned, in thirteen years of marriage, that you get into trouble assuming the worst. "He looks to be about twelve inches, though, legal enough, guess we'll just have to share him tonight."

She's still smiling as Hank bends down, picks the fish up by the stringer, lays it across the rock and with a knee on the fish to steady it, cuts off the head.

"Oh," she says, and sits. Sylvie has never seen this part of the fresh caught river dinners, savored before the fire on camp chairs, steaming in tin foil, shiny with buttered scallions and salt.

Hank quickly slits the fish from tail to missing head. With a deft scoop he eviscerates it and out plops a mass of multicolored, tunneled life topped by a still beating heart. With the knifepoint he motions toward a small pink heap. "Look, honey. See the eggs? It's a female." His knife chinks against the rock as he flicks the heaving mass of eggs closer for Sylvie to inspect. Two long rosy sacks swell and bulge with tiny pearls then taper to small threads. Not just a female, a mother-to-be.

Sylvie and Hank planned this long weekend on the Little River as their getaway, a second honeymoon, of sorts, at which they intended to relax, reconnect, and *reconceive*. Which isn't a word, of course, but they use it just the same. Not to friends, though, who can't bear to ask anymore, since their fourth and most recent loss occurred in the final trimester, no longer even a miscarriage, but a stillbirth. And it was *still* a birth: their perfectly formed, miniature son, lashes knitted together, arrived with all the attendant labor pains and follow-up bleeding. But what Sylvie remembers most is the eerie quiet of the labor room, and holding her tiny pewter baby in that deafening vacuum of sound.

And she remembers the milk. How it overflowed, two days after her empty-armed return from the hospital. Her ill-informed breasts, one step behind in the message chain—*thank you but we won't be needing your services after all.*

Sylvie shakes her head and looks back to the fish. She stares at the severed luminous green head, lips gaping around their shackle, mouth gasping soundless at impossible air. Bloody and bodiless, it lies on the rock as sun sparkles along the mottled jawline lush as a forest floor, dapples of silver sunlight and moss agate green.

The shimmery colors remind Sylvie of her little brother Luke and the magic mud they used to make as kids. Out behind the house at the shed where nothing grew they found the most amazing patch of ground. It first appeared in spring, after the blizzard of '77 when snow reached up to the roof at the little white house where they were born, near Niagara Falls, honeymoon capital of the world. Each time it rained that spring, their magic spot would sparkle with drips of color and glowing rainbows that ran through their hands like gloppy strands of pizza cheese.

That summer Sylvie turned twelve, still half-child herself, teetering on the cusp of outgrowing six-year-old Luke's games. In their childhood lore it became known as the hot rock summer. Mysterious bright blue rocks that exploded like pistol caps when you threw them onto concrete appeared in their backyard. They were cryptic moon rocks—weapons sent back from secret agent astronauts to fight an alien invasion. Luke loved those "hot rocks" and emptied a blue pocketful onto his bedside table every night.

And here, in the glistening mound of fish guts sit two remarkable blue shapes that wink up at her. What, inside a fish, could be blue?

"Here, honey, look," Hank says eagerly. "You can tell what he just ate. A crayfish." He holds up each blue pincher in turn to show her. "Cutting open the stomach and checking? That's my favorite part."

"*She*," Sylvie says and leans forward to pick up the tiny crayfish tail, perfectly preserved and neatly severed from the rest of its body, a Barbie lobster dinner. The fish must have captured and eaten the crayfish only moments before attacking Hank's lucky fly. There had been no time for digestion. And what had the crayfish eaten that morning which in turn might have been spared?

So much unnecessary loss of life.

"They love crayfish," Hank says, sawing through the flesh behind a ventral fin. The small armature of flexible bones crunches beneath the knife. "At least his last meal was a happy one."

"*Hers*," Sylvie says.

"Hmmm?" Hank looks up from the fish, confused. "Oh yeah, *hers*," he says and smiles. Sylvie has always loved Hank's smile. It's a movie star smile, even though Hank never gives his teeth a second thought. Good teeth were just one more thing that came naturally to Hank. Sylvie has dreams where rooms of children smile towards her, all wearing Hank's radiant grin.

She picks up the head of the fish and gently removes the metal clip, sliding it past the pink, feathered gills soft as rose petals. They spread and fan, choking on air that doesn't satisfy, air that goes nowhere. She strokes the silk-skinned jaw and slips the end of her pinkie inside the mouth, running it along a small spur of teeth.

"There's a lot of blood in the head," Hank says, "but not much anywhere else." Sylvie sees this. It's thick and dark red, stringy and disappointing like the menstrual blood that mocks her every month.

After Luke died it became even more important for Sylvie to have children, as if she hadn't wanted them enough before. But losing a brother who was nineteen to liver failure? And he the last male to carry on the family name? Well, it left her with a weighty emptiness, a whistling black void. And Sylvie longed to fill it. But her body refused. Or pretended to comply only to switch teams just when she thought she was home free.

First and foremost, there was the question of fault. *Whose systems have let us down?* Initially the doctors called it a simple failure to conceive. Then, when Sylvie conceived and lost, it became failure to sustain a pregnancy. And finally, after far too many losses and subsequent invasive probings, it was labeled a possible incompetent cervix. Sylvie did her sit-ups. She took extra folic acid. She stayed bedridden for days. For weeks she crossed her legs thinking, just stay in. Please stay in.

She was constantly reminded that there were women, women everywhere, who conceived effortlessly, recklessly. Women dismayed by the little plus sign on the stick, women who longed for a monthly crimson reassurance. Sylvie was haunted by the millions of cavalier abortions performed every day to rid these women of their burdens, when all she wanted was the *one*.

Worst of all, though, was the continuous roller coaster ride of hope and disappointment, the *please, please let me be* always followed by the *no, no not this time.*

The day the government bought their contaminated Love Canal home, they fled to Virginia's pristine bluegrass hills, and Sylvie has heard the constant ticking ever since, the corporeal time bomb that wakes her wide-eyed in the night, her very own tell-tale heart.

"Should I put it in the water?" Sylvie asks as she cradles the fish's pointed snout and rubs her thumb along the smooth skin below the eye.

"No, I'll bury it in the dirt when I'm done. Along with the entrails."

She dips the head in anyway and washes away tiny pebbled bits and pine scrubbings. The watery marbled eye peers upward at her through the silver surface. Sylvie shudders. "Can she see without her body if the brain is still attached?"

"Aw honey, don't worry. It's just a fish. He can't feel anything, I promise." Silver scales shed like shining raindrops as Hank scrapes from tail to head, sideways with the blade of his knife.

She, Sylvie thinks. *She* can't feel anything.

But Sylvie knows that sometimes it's the things you can't see or hear or feel that do the most damage. Likewise, the things that lull you into life: the place you lay your head at night, the sound of water flowing through its cycles, the shifting ground beneath your feet, the air you breathe.

Sylvie sets down the head to pick up the discarded ventral fin. She spreads it open like a fan. Thin ribs, webbed by a gossamer skin, open beneath her fingers. "It's a wing," she says, watching the veins open and close between her fingers. "Do they fly?"

"Sure," Hank says, smiling. "Smallmouth are really feisty and just leap right into the air. That's why they're so much fun to catch." He picks up the head and places the knife along the jaw, its point resting against the eye which rotates slightly from the pressure. "With a Smallmouth the jaw won't go past the eye. Largemouth bass go back a lot farther."

She nods, bringing the fin with its tiny piece of attached flesh to her nose and sniffing. "It smells sweet."

"Yeah, baby. Good eatin'. Course, later, your fingers won't smell so sweet. By this afternoon they'll be rank as a fish market." He lays down the head, flops the fish carcass over and begins scraping the other side as scales shower the surrounding rock, hit the surface of the water and float gently downward to lie sparkling along the bottom of the small pool of water.

He stands then, her husband, and folds up his knife, sliding the cleaned and gutted fish into a two-handled plastic grocery bag. He picks up the head and entrails in his other hand and maneuvers across the slippery faces of half-submerged rocks to the trail. Sylvie carries the rod. Just before they reach the dirt road where they have left the car Hank takes several steps to the side and drops the head and entrails into the surrounding weeds.

"I thought you were going to bury it?" she says.

"Yeah, well, it's been so long since we've had rain, the ground's too hard. It'll be fine, honey. Don't worry. Some animal will come along and eat what's left of him."

She watches his back as he pushes through the weeds at the end of the trail. His outline disappears from view as he steps out into the sunlit clearing.

"What's left of *her*," she says.

pygmalion (recast)

Steven counts the bills in his wallet one last time as he stands in line outside the museum. Fifty damn dollars to get in. He has the money, but wants to make absolutely sure before getting to the ticket window. He can't be turned away when he's made himself come this far, even though—given Ima's body donation—he *should* be let in free.

Clouds hover overhead; a misting rain beads on his anorak, dampening his khakis from the hips down. Ima loved inclement weather—and she'd have been pleased to stand in line, too. When the Cezanne exhibit came to Boston three years ago, the long lines had made her almost giddy.

Ima had always been the social one. Childlike, she was. Spontaneous. Engrossed by the simplest of things.

She told him once that the most difficult part of life modeling wasn't being naked in front of a group of staring, charcoal-poised artists, but rather standing like a dripping ice sculpture when what you most wanted to do was scratch your nose, or see what was happening in the next room. Steven understood; he had been the bemused husband who stood by while his easily distracted wife stared up into the pattern of a tree's underside branches, or circled a fountain to enjoy the satin slide of water slipping through her fingers.

Although she celebrated life, death fascinated Ima. Her mother died of ovarian cancer when Ima was seven, and two older half-brothers tormented her with tales of being buried alive, of cadaver-eating worms that ate a body from the inside out.

Two years, he'd read. Two years to get past the grieving. Two years to heal. But Steven thinks there must be a more complex equation than Death+2 years=Healing. Something that incorporates such factors as pain and love, years together and years denied.

Steven keeps his head down as the line advances. He doesn't want anyone he knows to see him here, doesn't want to have to explain this visit, doesn't want people searching his face to find the emotion they most want to see.

He eyes the ticket window as he approaches, half hoping to be turned away: a sign from the powers that be that he shouldn't have come.

"One," he tells the ticket taker when he reaches the window. If Ima were beside him she would lean forward and tell the man some small, humorous detail that would turn him into an instant friend.

"Fifty," the man says in reply.

Two: the sum of words that pass between them.

⌘

Steven first met Ima in the summer of '85, studying sculpture as a graduate student in Munich. She was twenty then—to his twenty-six—and she worked as the model for his life sculpture class. Her naked insouciance charmed him. His open admiration delighted her.

They toured the museums of the Kunstareal, starting with the Alte Pinakothek. There, Steven watched her study Rembrandt's *The Sacrifice of Isaac*. She stood transfixed by the angel flying in to stay Abraham's hand at the last moment, knife still falling through the air, Isaac lying prone on an altar of sticks, his father's hand covering his face as if unable to watch his son's dying expression, or to keep his son's last image from being that of a knife-wielding father. The sly-eyed ram (momentarily spared) gazing on from the middleground was Ima's favorite part of the painting. She said it was Rembrandt's private commentary on life's capriciousness.

They left that exhibit arm-in-arm, argued about art and immortality into the wee hours of the morning and then become lovers.

Ima joined Steven when he left Germany that fall. They moved to a converted barn where they learned that green wood doesn't burn hot and Maine winters are interminable. Steven taught painting, printmaking and sculpture at Bowdoin and Ima continued to model for him in class and at home. Images of Ima still covered the walls of his studio—charcoal, clay, bronze, gravure, oil—he had captured her in every medium and every pose. He never tired of reproducing her long, slender angles and Ima never tired of being immortalized.

Her father died in the summer of 2000 and they traveled back to Germany to help settle his affairs. The half-brothers fought bitterly over the estate and Ima left them to it, proclaiming *death brings out the worst in people.*

In Hamburg, freed of family obligations, they visited the city's art galleries and discovered a bizarre new touring show, part art, part science, part circus freak show. It was Worlds of the Body, an exhibit of preserved human remains, plastinated and posed, ostensibly for educating the public. Steven saw it as a desecration. Unable to secure a major public venue, the show was held in a small erotica museum in Hamburg's red light district across from the train station. Prostitutes and cab drivers were let in free.

Steven hadn't been able to get past the first three rooms. And that hot afternoon, waiting for Ima outside the Hamburg exhibit (an hour later she'd emerged, flushed and excited), they'd had their first argument on the subject of plastination.

"Oh, you should have stayed, Steven. It was amazing."

"Those were real bodies. People turned to—"

"Plastic," said Ima, sliding her arm through his.

"Exactly." He straightened his arm and let hers drop. "A freak show."

"It's edutainment, darling. It captivates you first, then it teaches you."

Radiant heat warped the tracks as Steven stared down their parallel lines, waiting on the train that would take them out of the city and back to the hostel. His pulse quickened and his palms began to sweat. The last exhibit he'd seen had been a carefully preserved sympathetic nervous system, twin nerves threaded to a pair of diminutive orange adrenal glands sitting atop their respective purple kidneys, poised to send a message: *Fight? Or flight?*

"It was repulsive."

"It was art, darling. Primal art."

He stared at her. "You'd do that?"

She stared back. "You can be such a prude, Steven."

He looked away. Ima's accusing stare burned the side of his face but he refused to turn. "I think you know I'm not a prude," he told the retreating tracks converging in the distance. Or were they arriving tracks, opening toward him? That was the hardest thing about perspective—understanding the relationship between things. "Just because I don't like the idea of thousands of people staring at my wife—what's left of my wife—" he rolled his shoulders.

"*Your* wife," she said with a dismissive wave. "People look at me all the time. Naked, even."

"That's different."

Ima raised an eyebrow.

"You're alive, for one thing. You're there because you want to be there. And—"

A distant whistle signaled the arriving train and mercifully ended their discussion.

⌘

Steven takes a deep breath and enters the exhibit hall. Thankfully there is no smell. Just an over-dry antiseptic quality to the air. The bodies and parts of bodies are odorless, truly plastic now. And the show begins innocently enough. The first exhibit is a skeleton. A real, human skeleton, yes, but who has not seen such a thing in high school biology? A skeleton is easy.

Three additional skeletons have successively greater bits of flesh and gore: nerves on the first, a fine network of white tendrils exiting the skull and spinal cord, connecting to various glands and organs; satiny-white ligamentous bands hold the bones together on the second; and the third supports the entire veinous system, suspended like red spider webs.

In the next room, a series of side-by-sides are exhibited: a healthy lung and a smoker's lung, a healthy liver and a cirrhotic liver, a normal heart and one with a reconstructed valve—graphic illustrations, all, of the risks we take and the damage we do, living and indulging. This, too, is easy to take, the sort of illustrated cautionary tale that humans have perfected and embraced for centuries.

⌘

The second argument occurred when Steven discovered donor information in Ima's stack of medical bills beside the fridge. It was a form, downloaded from the Internet that began, "Dear Sir or Madam, You are interested in the possibility of donating your body for plastination, a method of permanently preserving natural anatomical specimens for the purposes of research and instruction."

Specimens. Research. Instruction. It was infuriatingly clinical.

He'd snatched the paper up and gone looking for her. "What's this?" he said, thrusting it between Ima and the shirt she was ironing.

She looked at the paper, then at Steven, her face carefully expressionless. "Some information."

"I see that. Information for what?"

She sprayed starch on the collar before answering. "You see that, too, Steven, or you wouldn't be angry."

"I thought we talked about this." The smell of steam and starch filled the air. "You don't care what I think?"

"Steven, *liebling*, I care." She passed the iron back and forth, easing its point into the pleat of the yoke. "But it is my body."

"Your body that you won't need after…after you're gone."

"Dead, you mean. After I'm dead. You can say it, darling. And no, I won't need it. But neither will you. I don't want to be buried, to slowly rot, be eaten by worms. I couldn't die knowing that was waiting for me."

"Don't die, then. Stay."

"Everyone dies, Steven. Even you."

Her smiling, soft eyes made his temples throb. "We could be cremated and have our ashes mixed."

"You could be plastinated and posed with me."

He pressed his temples. "I don't want it for either one of us."

"But I do. I want my body to last. I want it to live on after the *me* part of me is gone. I want to travel the world like a mummified Egyptian queen. Be looked at forever and ever."

"God, Ima." He paced away from the ironing board, then turned and paced back. "Why couldn't you obsess about something simple, like religion? At least *that* would be easier to swallow."

She lifted a hanger from the end of the board and slid it into the shoulders of the shirt. "Easier to explain to your friends."

"You don't always have to be eccentric, you know. It isn't *expected* of you."

"I'll die—like my mother—but I won't be buried."

"You know I hate it when you talk like this. The oncologist said that with chemo—" he felt his face go hot and stopped.

Ima set the iron up on its end and took the paper from him. "An extra month. At most. A month of pain I don't want for either of us."

"Maybe *I* want the extra month."

"Not bald and suffering you don't. Not like that."

"I'll take you however. You know that."

"It's okay, Steven." She touched his arm but he shrugged it off.

"It's not okay." He stabbed the air with his finger. "It's not okay at all."

"It is, darling. You'll see. I'm not afraid if my body can be preserved."

⌘

Steven had never quite forgiven Ima—for the dying, yes, she couldn't help that, but not for the donation of her body. He wanted her remembered as she was in his paintings and drawings. *That* Ima, the living Ima, not dead Ima, not some ghoulish version of her. For that, his resentment would last longer than the plastinated heart on the *Worlds of the Body* posters he had seen around town for weeks.

At the entrance to the next room, two cantilevered torsos, side-by-side on a table, lean toward one another as if sharing a headless secret. They have been flayed to expose the internal organs and remind Steven, suddenly, of The Visible Man—an anatomy kit that, as a child, his older cousin owned and Steven coveted. It was a man, with skin of clear plastic, filled with a skeleton, blood vessels, and a set of multicolored internal organs that could be removed, examined, and neatly refitted. At the age of eleven, the toy had fascinated him and consumed his imagination for weeks. He begged to receive his own Visible Man for Christmas; his mother primly refused.

He steps through the doorway. The room is filled with partial specimens featuring arthritic joints and reconstructions. There is a child's skull with a metal plate fastened by screws and a grown man with a reconstructed jaw, red muscle fibers pulled away to reveal a line of interconnected silver track.

The ball-and-socket hip joint is beautiful, a gleaming engineering marvel. The reconstructed hip makes him think of his grandmother and then, perversely, of the still-living people surrounding him in the exhibit hall. If he had x-ray vision—another thing he coveted as a child—what marvels might he see beneath their skin?

Beside him, a young blonde woman leans forward. Her heavy floral perfume is overpowering and her knotted halter-top sways with a pair of heavy, obviously augmented breasts. What would she look like beneath her skin? Was she part way to plastination already?

Beauty, Steven thinks, is not merely skin deep, as the saying goes, but merely skin. And hair and nails and all the other outward trappings of humanness. And yet there is a strange sort of beauty to these skinless figures before him, these intricate, stripped-down mechanisms, these exquisitely designed parts of a greater machine.

⌘

"You could at least be happy that my final wishes will be honored." This time they argued across a two-person table in Mimesis, their favorite Boston bistro.

Steven shook his head. Discussing it in public increased the pain of Ima's after-death decision.

She leaned forward onto her elbows. "I'm not doing it just for me, you know. If people can see ovarian tumors—how small and harmless they look at first—and then see me, right in front of them, dead from the tumors…if even one woman pays attention to the symptoms and gets treatment because of that, well, I've helped."

"You do realize how ironic it is for you to talk about treatment when you've refused everything the doctors have suggested." He straightened his knife and fork.

"Don't be angry, darling."

"What should I be? Happy?" He took a sip from his sweating water glass; his hand shook.

"Proud of me. I'm using my death to help others."

"So you are *unselfishly* putting money into this Dr. Frankenstein's pocket. How very altruistic of you, Ima."

"Visitors leave his exhibits determined to value their bodies. Smokers walk away, leaving their cigarettes behind."

The waitress arrived bearing two bowls of clam chowder that she set before them. Steven nodded curtly and continued. "So he's P.T. Barnum and Florence Nightingale all rolled into one. I still don't want Saint Frankenstein making a profit off your death."

"An undertaker would. Profit from my death." Ima pointed to the bread. "Butter me?" When Steven picked up the knife she continued. "Anyway, I don't care about that. It's about immortality. And art. The doctor is an artist, like you, only his medium *is* the human body. He's a modern day Pygmalion who flips the myth and turns real people into sculptures." She watched him spread the softened butter. "Lots, please."

"It's gruesome. Macabre. A story by Poe." He set the bread on the edge of her plate.

"Darling, da Vinci dissected cadavers—to see the underpinnings of the body, to understand its movement. The practice is centuries old." She ran her finger through the butter and placed the tip in her mouth.

Steven shook his head. "Don't lecture me, Ima. Not about Leonardo." This was not a rational dilemma that needed discussing. It was a gut reaction that needed respecting: *Don't dissect my wife.*

"You Americans are so afraid of death."

"Oh, here we go, the *You Americans* speech again."

"Well you are, my dearest. Europeans know death more intimately. We are not so afraid of the body failing. We know it is part of life. What's the painting by Rembrandt? I know you know this. The Anatomy Lesson of Dr. Something-or-other."

"Tulp. Dr. Nicholaas Tulp." Steven did remember it, a masterpiece of group portraiture and chiaroscuro: the anatomists lean in, eagerly surrounding the white-bodied corpse, its flayed forearm the centerpiece as the doctor uses forceps to move the tendons, simultaneously demonstrating with his other hand. Steven taught this painting to his students.

"Before Rembrandt could paint his natural bodies, he had to know *how* they moved." She took a bite of bread, retrieving a dangling bit of butter with her tongue.

⌘

In the fourth room of the exhibit hall, Steven finds full bodies, posed with a nod to familiar artworks and attitudes. There is The Thinker, a seated blood vessel man studying a decapitated head on the table before him; a flayed man, holding his own skin, draped over his forearm; a man, seated at a chess board, contemplating his next move, his skull opened and his brain exposed; and a man kneeling in an attitude of prayer, holding his heart in his hands.

There are fewer female bodies: a woman, swimming, splits in half down the middle and swims off in two directions, another poses on-point like a Degas ballerina, her flayed abdominal muscles her tutu, and a third sits cross-legged, nursing her plastinated baby at a plastinated breast. Just when he is ready to leave in frustration and disgust, Steven sees the blood-vessel family, parents holding hands, a small child atop the father's shoulders. They resemble ghosts, human outlines draped with red lace, beautiful in the threading feathery bright-red manner of our vesicular systems, and their tiniest arteries visually melt into one another till the ends are indistinguishable. Blood, they seem to be saying, binds us together.

⌘

"There will be advantages, you know," Ima said, one of the last nights she was lucid, continuing the argument without preamble, home in bed. The pain had progressed and a morphine pump had been installed. In normal life, Ima had eschewed drugs, resisted all attempts at medication. But the cancer had given her permission, of sorts, and she used her morphine liberally.

"I wish you wouldn't talk about this now." He sat cross-legged at the foot of the bed, making a quick pencil sketch while Ima read. He was drawing her every day now, at least once, hoping to stay her physical deterioration with the power of his pencil—document the destruction, freeze it, pin it down.

The skin beneath her eyes was darkening and sinking. Her lips had thinned. Her neck looked longer, an elegant Modigliani. She turned a page in *Death with Dignity*.

"How can you read such morbid stuff?"

"You won't have to pick out a casket," Ima said, ignoring his question.

"You really are cruel, you know that?" He smudged a shadow on her cheek with the side of his thumb.

"There won't be a plot to maintain."

He flipped the page over, even though he hadn't finished the sketch, and rifled loudly through his box of pencils.

"And you can visit me whenever you want. I will be *rescued from decomposition*."

He set the sketchpad on his knees and looked at her. She lay back against her pillows wearing a dreamy expression, arms over her head, thinning hair spread against the pillow.

"You'll always know where to find me, *liebling*."

⌘

By the end of the show—with only one room left to visit—Steven hasn't recognized any exhibit that could be Ima. She requested a full-body plastination, but the consent forms specified that the doctor reserved the right to use donated bodies in whatever way he felt best served the public knowledge and his need for plastinates. Signing that assurance away had been Ima's only reservation. She didn't want to be displayed in pieces.

The final exhibit has a room all its own. He hesitates before entering. His palms are sweating and he wipes them on his khakis. What if she isn't here? *What if she is?*

He rounds the corner and inside, in the middle of the room, is the sole exhibit: a female body, a reclining Odalisque posed on a plush velvet pillow with her abdomen flayed and her reproductive organs exposed. With all the fat and skin removed, the hips are thin and the legs rangy. The overhead fluorescent lights are bright, too, no hint of chiaroscuro, no dramatic highlighting, no artful obscuring.

This human sculpture has no hair, no skin, no outer trappings of a human. But the inner woman is there for all to see. The uterus is smaller than a fist, cross-sectioned to show the lining. Two fallopian tubes hover above the ovaries like hungry question marks, feathery, grasping fingers eternally waiting for an egg. The left ovary is small, an egg-shaped mass, lumpy and white except for the first stage tumors covering it, highlighted spots of bright pathology-yellow, they look like the bumps on raw chicken skin.

The right ovary, the one that the doctors said "went first" is a hideous pulpy mass. It dwarfs the normal ovary, the uterus, everything around it. And, God help him, Steven thinks it looks more like the General Tso's chicken they ordered every Friday from the take-out place down the street than anything else. It isn't tidy or dainty, but glistening and crispy-fried.

Steven stands and stares. Fellow museumgoers part, divide ranks around him, and reconnect on the other side. The small placard attributes the plastinated body to *a woman in her forties who died of ovarian cancer*. A list of symptoms follows.

Ima would have liked the idea of being an Odalisque in death, Manet's *Olympia* her favorite—the model, infamously depicted staring naked and immodest from the frame. Ima would have liked to warn other women, remind them to *pay attention to the signs*. She would have approved of the list, and of the plush, tasseled cushions.

Steven briefly conjures an image of his own body placed within the exhibit, also plastinated, standing at an easel, painting Ima. They could be their own still life, artist and model, forever frozen in the attitudes that made them happiest, adorer and adored.

A woman who has been standing beside Steven bumps his arm when she turns to leave. The physical contact brings him back to the moment, back to the brightly lit room. "Pardon me," he says and steps to the side.

"It's okay," she tells him over her shoulder as she walks away. Her high-heeled shoes provide a distant staccato clack. The words hang in the air. *It's okay.*

Steven takes a deep breath and reaches into the pocket of his anorak. He retrieves his charcoal pencil and small everyday sketchpad. *It's okay.* He places the pencil between his teeth and flips through dozens of Ima sketches until he finds an empty page.

model home

Even as a child, Kelly never liked mirrors. While other children might spend hours staring into mirrors, trying on faces for impact, watching themselves in tragic fascination as they cried, or gazing open-mouthed into their own half-chewed food, Kelly never did. Mirrors had always seemed traitorous to her, suspiciously dormant; a liquid, shining eye, like mercury that might at any moment part and suck her through.

So coming across a split-level home of mostly mirrors on her honeymoon house-hunting tour didn't thrill Kelly. She and Andrew had researched hundreds of houses via the Internet during their four-week, long-distance engagement, emailing house descriptions and pictures back and forth. Those virtual images had held such promise, each one a world of possibilities. But the day Kelly drove across Virginia—from Kentucky-bordered coal country to Eastern Shore crab country—to view the houses, she found a wide discrepancy between the photo-descriptions and reality.

And as near as she can remember, none of the computer listings had mentioned a house with mirrored walls, and yet here she was, confronted, the moment she stepped in, by floor-to-ceiling paneled mirror strips, a pair of fully mirrored sliding closet doors, and a mirrored, tiled ceiling overhead. The entire foyer sparkled when the chandelier was lit.

"What's with all the mirrors?" Kelly asked Andrew as they fell in step behind the real estate agent.

"Mm?"

"The mirrors," she said, grabbing his arm and speaking into his ear. "Lots and lots of mirrors."

"I'd like you to see the downstairs first," the agent said, speaking over her shoulder as they descended the stairs, reflected selves keeping pace in the mirrored wall to their left. "The master bedroom is through here," she said, holding her arm out towards an odd square area—half hallway, half room—off of which a bathroom, bedroom and basement exited.

Two-inch, square, mirror tiles covered the ceiling, fragmenting Kelly's reflection into a cubist portrait when she looked up. Beside her, a mirrored wall, oddly studded by a double tier of Tru-life makeup lights, reflected the three remaining walls, also mirrored, complete with mirror moldings, mirror switch plates, and mirror outlet covers.

"The former owner was a model," said the agent. "This is where she did her make-up."

"A model?" said Andrew. "That explains a lot."

"Would we know her?" asked Kelly.

"Oh, sure. She was a super model in the eighties. Her face was everywhere. Donna Regis."

"Donna Regis?" said Andrew. "Sorry, no."

"But surely you know of her," said the agent. "She was discovered right down the street working at Howe's drugstore when she was sixteen. Then she was a cover girl and sold that line of clothing and advertised for Feed the World."

"We're not from around here," offered Kelly.

"No? Well, maybe that's why," said the agent. "But still." She led them back upstairs to a formal sitting area with a rock fireplace and large picture window, surrounded on either side by mirrored vertical blinds. To the right, a large dining area appeared at first to be two rooms, until Kelly realized that the other room had the three of them standing in it as well. "Where are you from then?"

"I've been in D.C. for twelve years," said Andrew, "but the FBI just moved operations to Quantico so we thought we'd look around here."

"And we just got married," said Kelly, linking her arm into Andrew's.

⌘

The six months during which Kelly had tried computer dating before she met Andrew on-line had proven that—description or no— you had to see the product in person before you could believe the claims. Computer dating wasn't her first choice for meeting men, but in Grundy, Virginia, the dating prospects weren't exactly abundant and interesting. And through the anonymity of the Internet, men who would ordinarily take years to reveal themselves in person gave away intimate details with each musical trill of the incoming instant message screen. Fortunately, Kelly enjoyed weeding out men at the speed of light that way. No-risk male browsing was the ultimate shopping thrill.

Most of all, though, Kelly knew she didn't want to end up an old maid teacher caring for her aging mother, or worse, leading a cars-on-blocks existence in a trailer on the edge of a mountain. She knew, from the death of her parents' marriage, to be careful. Kelly hated to think of her mother during those infidel years: staring out darkened windows muttering declarative statements of hate and bravado, checking pockets for little folded-paper bombs, engaging her father in late-night scream sessions rank with accusation and tearful pleading. Worse, though, was how traitorous Kelly felt for still loving her father, for dressing up, flirting, and preening to keep him home; then, when he wouldn't stay, feeling inadequate, and angry, as if he were cheating on her, too.

For Kelly, the effect of those years had always been physical. At ten years old she lay in bed and plucked her hair out, strand by soothing strand, until her mother discovered a bald patch the size of a silver dollar and spanked her soundly. At twelve she sucked a blood-bruise onto her forearm and chewed the skin of her fingertips down to raw pink dermis. No one understood what a comfort it was to exercise control over something as wild and capricious as a body.

When she told Andrew these stories, he wasn't shocked. He said that was what he loved about her—her intensity. Andrew had proven the calm exception to the flock of odd and desperate Internet men. She came across him, miraculously, on the same day she logged in, disgusted, to remove her personal profile from the cyber meat market. She had begun a final browse of the "men currently on-line" page when a screen name popped up with a pair of hearts entwined, indicating a personal profile that matched hers. When she clicked on his picture, and it opened up before her, all three-piece suit and salt-and-pepper goatee, she trembled with anxious desire.

At 45, Andrew, admittedly a little old, was still quite the catch: stable, never married, with a government job and a condo in D.C. When she first spoke to him on the phone, his voice was deep and rich; they talked for hours until her ears were hot and sore. He laughed in all the right places with a warm chuckle that made her want to crawl up inside his chest and feel it vibrate all around her.

Andrew came to meet Kelly that first weekend, drove six hours each way, just to have lunch with her and meet her mother. He was the first man she'd ever met who knew exactly what he wanted. Decisive, that was the word for Andrew. He called her "fresh" and "hot" and said he knew the moment he saw her that he had finally met the woman he would marry. Within a month he was suggesting they elope to Vegas, and within three months, they had.

Kelly began calling Andrew her "make-it-happen man" the day they bought the house. After hours of entering musty smelling fixer-uppers, chip-strewn bachelor pads, and remodeled-for-the-aged-grandmother homes, he said he knew the house was destined to be theirs the moment he stepped across the threshold. Built in the 1960s, impeccably maintained, it even had new appliances and spotless beige carpeting. It smelled good. If not for the mirrors, it would have been perfect.

⌘

"We live in the house of a thousand mirrors," said Andrew, on their first night as homeowners.

"Yeah," said Kelly, lifting a leg and kicking the air. "And when I do this? It's like being with the Rockettes."

"Ooh, now that has possibilities." He stroked his jaw in appraisal.

"Except I'm hardly built for a chorus line." Kelly stood tall and smoothed her hands down her shirt, drawing in her stomach and pulling her shoulders back. "Too much bounce in the breasts."

"Never."

"Good answer, honey." She blew Andrew a kiss then leaned against the bathroom counter and lifted her chin toward the mirror. "You know, these makeup lights show every last pore. Why would anyone design a home where you can't get away from yourself?"

"They brighten the place up. We get twice the light."

"God, you sound like the realtor. I think they're creepy. Who would ever want to see themselves so much?"

"Relax. Once we're settled I'll take out some mirrors. It's no big deal."

"No big deal to you. You never look back. God, I can't believe we have a house. I think I'm getting hives."

"Hives?" Andrew flattened a box and stepped on it, watching Kelly's reflection in the mirror as he did so.

"You must admit the whole meet-marry-move-buy-a-home thing has been a tad stressful," she said, concentrating as she spread toothpaste across the bristles of her toothbrush.

"Stressful? You've left Podunk, USA, you don't need to work, and you live in a gorgeous house. How's that stressful?"

She turned to face him, pointing with her toothbrush. "The *speed* of it was stressful." She began to brush her teeth with short, vigorous strokes.

Andrew shrugged. "I know a deal when I see one."

"Yesh, I know. You were helpesh to reshist," she said, catching a drip of toothpaste with her hand.

"Well, I don't like to let the good things get away." He passed her a creased and flattened towel from the opened box marked *linens*. "I snatched *you* up, didn't I?"

She spit into the sink and cupped her hand under the running water. "Out of the very jaws of death, honey."

⌘

When Kelly picked Andrew up from work the next day, he climbed into the car with a heavy sigh. "Bad news," he said without preamble, punctuating it with the click of his seatbelt buckle.

"Okay." Kelly leaned over to kiss him thinking *the first bad news of our marriage*. "I'll bite. What's up?"

"The Bureau is sending me to Thailand." He spoke in a resigned monotone and didn't look at her.

"Thailand?" She tightened her grip on the wheel. "Jeez. Why Thailand?"

"More remains." He passed a hand down his face.

"God. How many?"

"Possibly three. Who knows? It's just fragments. A downed Huey." Andrew leaned over and adjusted the briefcase at his feet. "This isn't my choice, you know."

"I know," said Kelly, touching his arm. "For how long?"

"Three months."

"Three *months?*" She drew her hand back.

He looked at Kelly for a long moment while she drove and glanced from the road to him and back. "We've discussed this, Kell. It's my job."

"Well I know, I know. But three *whole* months? That's as long as we've known each other."

"Look, the Bureau says, 'Jump,' I say, 'How high?'"

"But why for so long?"

"Three months isn't that long, Kelly. It's not simple body recovery. It's a twenty-five-year-old crash site in the middle of the freaking jungle—which obliterates everything. The bodies, if they ever were intact, have been picked over by animals, or people, strewn around, and you can bet the chopper's been stripped of any useful parts. Retrieving remains means a week, minimum, to get in-country and on-site in the first place, then you sort through the wreckage, down to sifting dirt if necessary. The remains have to be sorted and classified . . . it's endless, really. Three months is just a starting figure."

"Okay, okay, I get it. You're going. You have to go. But it still *sucks*."

"In a word, yes."

"Can I go with you?" She hated the pleading sound of her own voice.

"Don't I wish you could."

"Well I can. Why not? I'm not teaching anymore. I've got time."

"Kelly, dependants aren't authorized or even allowed on these missions. You know that. Besides, we couldn't go away and leave the house for three months."

"Well *you* are," she said, staring him down at a stoplight. "Leaving, I mean."

He pointed her back to the now-green light. "My job pays the bills. I don't have a choice."

"So, apparently, neither do I." In the silence that followed, Kelly had the feeling of sitting inside her mother's pinched, resentful skin, and changed her tone. "Okay, fine. I'll be here and you'll be there. But we'll talk, right?"

"Sure we will. Every day I can manage it. And we'll email, too. Just like old times."

"Old times?" She turned the car into the driveway and looked at him. "What old times?"

⌘

Kelly dropped Andrew and his duffels at the airport and drove home with a wretched swelling in her throat. There had been so little time. And very little warning, like her father's unexpected leaving, so many years ago. Her mother's howling grief and anger then had negated Kelly's own, and at fifteen she had struggled not to feel the same desperate drowning desire to leave that she knew her father must have felt. So she used her skin to provide relief, a simple regaining of control. A scab, picked slowly, just-so, a cuticle, torn gently, lengthwise with the grain of flesh, created the perfect stinging antidote to keep despair at bay.

Kelly's chest tightened. As she drove, she pinched the skin of her wrists to be sure she was alive. She would not let herself think about husbands and fathers going away.

As Kelly opened the front door and entered the empty house, the movement of her own reflection in the mirrored foyer startled her; she would never get used to the constant reflected motion. And good God, look at her: purse dragging at her side, her hair a mess, her wrists a mass of reddening pinch marks, her face thick with unspilled tears. No wonder Andrew left. She'd go away, too, if only she could escape her own disgusting self.

Kelly turned her back to the mirrors, lay on the floor, and sobbed. How would she ever manage? *Just like a man to leave her high and dry.* What would Andrew do there, alone, so far away? *Cheat, obviously. It's what they all did.* How could he leave her like this? *He didn't even care.* Why wasn't she enough to make him stay?

The light from the windows changed to a dusky purple and Kelly's tears turned to salty smudges. A dry longing sat at the back of her tongue. She eased herself up stiffly and stretched. Andrew was gone. There was nothing to be done about that. She stepped forward until her toes met the mirror, and standing close, pointed to her reflected image. She made a stern face. "Kelly Swank, you will make the best of living here. You will learn to appreciate these mirrored walls. You will save on paint. You will have lots of reflected light. You will buy Windex by the case."

To prove her change of heart she would give the mirrors some loving care, spray off the smudgy streaks of moving day, of dusty coveralls and sweaty hands. It would keep her mind and body occupied, and show the house her good intentions.

Downstairs, in the area outside the bathroom, she stared into a mirrored wall, holding her left hand, with its diamond-studded wedding ring, beside her face and looking into her fixed, red-rimmed eyes. With her other hand she lifted the spray bottle, took aim, and shot her reflection in the face.

As she sprayed and wiped, she studied herself in the various mirrors. How could she not? There was no looking *through* a mirror. And every time she turned around, there she was. Kelly, Kelly, everywhere. Clearly, it was time to make some changes if she hoped to keep her husband. For starters she would lose that extra fifteen pounds.

And that night, Kelly pleased herself by eating only a bagel for dinner. Then, while waiting for the call from Andrew that never came, she tweezed her eyebrows into two thinly arched lines. It took over an hour. Each mincing pain above her eye was pure pleasure. She had to force herself to stop.

⌘

The following day when Kelly was searching for twine to tie a stack of crushed boxes for recycling, she came across a magazine clipping in the far corner basement drawer. She pulled it out and studied it for signs of recognition; a manicured face (smooth even skin, piled curls of hair, straight white teeth in a practiced smile) stared back. Kelly took a moment to think of this woman in this house, then ran the image through the copier twice and taped one picture to each bathroom mirror. The original she stuck to the fridge and Donna Regis's flawless face smiled coolly out, a single line of text under the photo urging, "Eat to Live. Don't Live to Eat."

⌘

When Andrew finally called, more than a week into his trip, the staticky connection gave Kelly a sense of panic. How would she remember to say everything she'd been thinking? How could she tell him that his absence left her groundless, floating, and sore? How would she manage to be funny and charming, yet needy enough that he would be compelled to call again?

"How are you?" shouted Andrew from the other side of the world.

"I'm good." *Be cheerful.* "But I miss you." *And inquire into his life.* "How are you?"

"Good, good. I'm good. How's the house?"

"It's good. The mirrors are starting to get to me though."

Andrew laughed a hearty laugh that should have been a comfort, but wasn't. "Oh, you'll do fine, honey. Just ignore them."

Kelly had tried this. But in that fraction of a second between instinct and reason, when each reflected movement caught the edge of her eye, she couldn't help feeling that someone was there, someone was watching her. Try as she might, she couldn't force her thinking brain to override that first instinctual burst of panic that fractured her days into blasts of unwelcome adrenaline.

"Listen, I've got to run, Kell, but I'll call you again soon, okay?"

"Soon is good." *Don't nag.*

He laughed again. "All right, honey, point taken."

"Andrew? Wait!"

"Yes?"

"What about email?" *Don't beg.*

"Oh, a connection is ridiculously expensive to get here, but I'll try to send one this week. Gotta run, honey. Love you."

"All right. You, too." And he was gone. She held the phone away from her ear and stared at the black receiver in her hand.

Afterward Kelly lay in bed thinking of all the things she should have said, could have said, would have said if she'd had more time. She should have asked how the recovery was going, who else was on the job with him, if they had identified the bodies, if the weather was holding, if the women were beautiful. She struggled to stop picturing Andrew, dark and handsome, drinking-in the decadence of Thailand—the Thailand she had read about, where Viagra sold cheap, by the handful, on street corners. Where ridiculously young and desperate girls serviced men under the tables in sex cafés while the men folded their newspapers, talked and sipped their beers above the lipsticked bobbing heads, the sluicing hands, pretending that their minds weren't being blown beyond belief at their own good fortune.

Kelly shook her head, slapped her cheeks and sat up. The house was too quiet. She hated being alone with herself. Too much solitude made her heart perform a desperate skipping dance. She turned on the TV and searched through the late night infomercials for company. And there, on channel 82, a familiar face smiled dryly out at her. Donna Regis, beautiful and aloof, stood before the camera exhorting Kelly to feed the hungry children of Bangladesh. Kelly stared in fascination at the angular shoulders, the hollow cheekbones and long thin neck. Donna Regis looked exquisite, a starving child of Bangladesh herself, beautiful and doomed.

Kelly located the box she had packed in her own Grundy bathroom three weeks earlier and dug through it. She found the hair color, lightener, actually, that her mother had purchased a year earlier and given to Kelly in one of her many attempts to make her more man-friendly. On a whim Kelly had packed it for the move, intending to use it as a prop to regale Andrew with one of her can-you-believe-my-mother stories. No matter, there it was, just when she needed it.

While the *gentle botanicals of aloe, chamomile, and ginseng* seeped into her hair Kelly shaved her legs. The entire leg, from toe to hip— something she had known for a while that other women did, but had not done her self. After a moment's hesitation Kelly soaped her forearms and shaved them, too. The rivulets of water flowing down her hair-free skin sent shivers of pleasure throughout her body. As she rinsed away the long soft arm hairs, the razor's polished edge shone with a beckoning gleam. Several hairs remained lodged between the twin blades of the razor. Kelly swiped it sideways across her forearm to remove them and a hairline slice of skin began to fill satisfyingly with red.

To avoid breakfast, Kelly rewashed her newly lightened hair, then blow-dried it and carefully curled it all over. At noon, a woman Kelly didn't recognize came to the door and knocked, then peered in, her face moon-white and pressed against the window, hands to either side of her eyes. Kelly stood and watched her, twice-reflected from the bathroom door, but did not move.

By dinner, Kelly decided that food was a weakness she couldn't afford to indulge this day. She was purifying, tearing down and building anew, and as the hours passed she realized that sleep, too, was a simple and absurd notion—something for those of a lesser constitution.

Yet there was still much to do. Kelly would keep improving. She would make herself into a trimmer, more beautiful woman. She would polish her nails and wear high heels. She would make her husband proud. Then Andrew would come home.

One look, and he would never leave her side again.

⌘

As the sun begins to rise, the new Kelly is not hungry. She is not hungry, yet she realizes that to live one must eat. She does not want to *die*. And so she cuts a piece of bread and saves one half for later. Then, thinking better of it, she saves three-quarters of the bread for later. She places the remainder in a bowl and cuts it into tiny pieces.

From her spot on the refrigerator door, Donna Regis fixes Kelly with a disapproving stare. The children of Bangladesh are starving, yet Kelly eats.

Only today Kelly cannot eat. The bread is coarse and inedible. With a sharper steak knife she cuts the pieces smaller and yet each bite grows inside her mouth, sawdusty dry and swelling with saliva until it fills her jaws with a gagging sigh and chokes her. Kelly runs to the bathroom, knife in hand, and retches up her food. It is only so much dirt.

A throbbing pain pounds inside her head. Like a TV on the fritz, she whacks it on the side. The pain moves in swirling eddies that want out, that whirl and suck her down, spinning a roily sludge that would pull her skin and hair away, peel her down to nothing.

She only wants to let it out.

Kelly holds the fine, sharp point of the steak knife poised above her inner forearm. She brings the handle down with enough force to split the skin and a small amount of pain escapes like hissing steam. She sighs.

Her body vibrates with a low throbbing pulse and the bright cosmetic lights glint along the silver edge of the knife as she lowers the blade and carefully cuts. The skin of her arm resists at first, pressing down beneath the blade, rising up on either side. Then she places the knife within the tiny split and slides it slowly across her arm. Her skin gives way, and a grinning wet red gash stretches across her arm. There is no pain—it takes the other pain away, in fact, and makes her feel alive.

She makes another sliding cut below the first, and a satisfying drip travels from one cut to the next then gathers and slides down her arm. One drop falls like a ruby into the sink, beautiful against the bright enamel.

Kelly takes a deep breath and smiles. If only she had known it was this simple all along.

She wipes the knife clean then wraps a towel around her arm and hums. She turns off the 16 Tru-life makeup lights and steps out of the bathroom into semi-darkness.

Her eye catches the movement of a figure in front of her and she freezes in sudden terror, hands in mid-motion. She stands there, caught and startled, face-to-face with a stranger—this unfamiliar person who has snuck into her house to harm her.

the rashomon tree

Pearl

If my momma taught me one thing, she taught me about God. I know about paradise lost. I know we was all put here to rule over God's creations. To anyone who has ever read the Bible, it's plain enough—God wants us to take charge of this world He gave us. He didn't make it in six days out of dust and nothing and finish up with us in His likeness, only to have us shirk being in charge. It is one of our divine responsibilities. Take Adam for instance. He had to name every single animal God gave him. Now there's a job for you. Or Noah, being responsible for saving all them animals and keeping them healthy on a ark for such a long spell. Can you imagine what that ark must've smelled like? I'd like to see some of them Greenpeace folks try and do what Noah did.

Henna

When I was 30, my body turned upon itself. Diabolical rogue cells invaded my tissues, gobbling up the good in a slow, inexorable advance. It was for me, as it is for many, life-altering. In the daily grind of surviving I grew stronger—Amazonian: one breast gone, ready for battle.

Now, I take nothing for granted. My life has become one of purity and balance, in sustainable harmony with nature, embracing the teachings of Siddhartha Gotama and the spirit of Gaia. I believe all creatures, with or without a beating heart, have a soul. The plants, flowers, and trees all breathe, eat, and grow the same as you or I— motility has never been the quintessence of life.

My own near death gave me a finer appreciation for life, and although I do not now, nor have I ever, needed a man in my life, I was able to find one, whom I respected, willing to help me bear a child. The delightful product of that brief union was Sky, light of my life, joy of my days.

Pearl

It was just a tree. A big old half-rotted tree with worrisome leaves that stuck in your rake so's you could hardly get down to the grass. You know the kind. A worry and a bother is all.

I pride myself on my lawn. It's the nicest lawn in the whole county. And I have got animals besides. There's the prettiest little squirrel stuck on the trunk of my dogwood tree, and the cutest baby bunny you ever saw in front of my azalea bushes. Some people, Buelah Roberson for instance, put such tacky animals in their yard, like chickens, and a pelican. Poor thing, she don't have a bit of style.

My best animals is three big geese. The brown ones with the black head, like in that movie *Fly Away Home*. Jeff Daniels was so good in that. They are real pretty. I had to go all the way to Grandfather Mountain to find them. One has its head down looking for food and the other two look like they could just walk right off any second. I move them around so they don't sit in the same spot all the time. Why just the other day, Preacher Pratt was saying how my yard makes him look every time he drives by.

Sky

There's a hole in the ground that a tree left. I put a peanut butter pinecone on it for the birds. Then it got cut down. I stood still as a statue and a little one with a black head ate a sunflower off my mitten.

Henna

When Pearl first approached me about the ancient oak tree between our houses, I told her in no uncertain terms that I did not want that majestic tree cut down. Just watching the men from Appalachian Power Company trim a few branches last fall was painful enough. The white circles of raw wood left behind in place of her beautiful boughs were like amputated stumps. A tree as old as her deserves respect. Since the day I moved here, she has towered over this yard, offering shade and solace, quietly comforting, protecting, and sheltering us from the elements, embodying the great Mother Creator herself.

In autumn the terminal ends of her boughs weighed heavy with acorns. Little Sky would gather them by the bucketful, plink, plunk, plunk. One by one he picked them up and admired the nutty chestnut colors and rounded shapes, the very essence of fecundity itself.

In the bleak days of February, her stark, stolid body set against the gunmetal gray of winter sky gave me hope of life's renewal— made me calm in the assurance of life after winter.

In April, she unfolded pastel, soft, sweet baby leaves followed by tassels of yellow pollen to adorn the world with dusts of gold.

As summer approached, the birds would court, then nest and raise their young outside our windows. A handmade wooden birdhouse—Sky's first painting project, a splash of bright colors— hung on her lowest branch. Every spring the same pair of wrens returned to raise a brood. We watched the mother wren coax her babies out, by turns calling sweetly, then scolding harshly in her scare-away-the-cat voice. I felt a kindred spirit as I watched her struggle with the inevitable push and pull of motherhood, of guiding her babies to independence.

I don't even know where that birdhouse is, now. Taken for firewood along with the rest of her, I suppose.

Pearl

It's hard enough to do my yard without a tree full of acorns, dead branches, noisy woodpeckers and squirrels always dropping something on you. That tree was a nuisance, what with all the mess and critters. Lord, I even saw a black snake go up the side of it once! I'd have cut it down years ago if it wasn't half in the neighbor's yard. But do you think I could have ever got *Ms. Starchild* to agree? Not hardly. Now, don't get me wrong. She's a sweet girl and all, and I'm not one to gossip, or anything, love thy neighbor as thyself, I always say. But I just don't see how someone who goes to court to change her Christian name to Starchild, and her given name to Henna, has a baby without a man, then up and names the child Sky, can keep a proper yard. You should see it. It's shameful the way she lets it go, and an embarrassment to me. It just makes me sick to have it set right up next to my pretty white fence and careful lawn. Why my husband said to me just last week, "Pearl," he said, "I don't know how you stood that tree as long as you did, all the trouble it has caused you. You have got the patience of Job."

And he's right, I do. For years I put up with squirrels making ragged, nasty nests, and springtime birds that would scream and fight for a spot in that tree. Lord, it liked to wake the dead. And in the middle that ice storm—winter past, I mean—a big old half-rotted limb broke off and took 16 shingles off my roof. You can see why I couldn't stand the old thing.

Sky

People shouldn't fight about stuff like trees. They should just grow.

Henna

I let her down. Incredibly strong, and seemingly invincible, still she needed me to protect her. She had no means to run away or defend herself. In a true contest, man against tree, no weapons save his hands and her bark, she would have won, leaves down. But against the tools of technology—chain saws spitting smoke and fire, stump eaters chewing the last of her roots into a muddy-white sawdusty pile—she was defenseless. Like the monks who immolated themselves to protest Vietnam, she stood there and quietly died as they dismembered her.

Of course, if I had been there, it never would have happened. They would have had to pass their chain saws through my body to get to hers. But Sky and I were not there, of course. We were in

California visiting my sister. We calculated the days and surmised that our tree breathed her last on the day of our whale-watching cruise. And so we were admiring the great behemoths of the sea while our own precious ancient was being struck down. Pearl swears she had no idea we would care, but she knew enough to do it while we were away.

Pearl

I swan. I've half a mind to go and give that woman her part of the bill. It's not as if money grows on—well, you know. But I don't because I am a good Christian woman who tries hard to live by God's laws—unlike some people around here. Why, Ms. Starchild has got herself a fat little naked Buddha man in her front yard for anybody to see. Her purple car, *not* USA made, says things like "Keep your laws off my body," "Proud to be a Being In Total Control of Herself" and, on its back bumper, "Goddess Power." Lord only knows what that woman means to say with them. I hate to think of it, I do.

When she first moved in next door I wasn't exactly happy, having a unwed mother and all as a next-door neighbor. But I did as the Lord instructs us. I made up my special Jell-O lemon cake and took it over to her.

She was nice enough; I'll give her that. Said her name was Henna, and that boy of hers was Sky. Said their last name was Starchild. So I asked her, what name is *Starchild*, German or French, or what have you, and she said it was a made-up name, she reckoned, and good as any.

"Didn't you have a father?" I asked.

"Why certainly, but where do you suppose his name came from?" she said.

Well, first off, I don't much care for a person to speak to me like I am child, which I am not, but I swallowed and said, "From his father, I'm sure. Just the same as I come from a long line of Vests."

"Pearl Vest?"

"Yes'm. Up until the day I met and married Cecil," I told her. "After that I was proud to be a Goad."

Henna

I think it behooves you to know that although I found Pearl a bit backwards and odd, I did not treat her any differently because of it. In the beginning, you might even say we were friends. Pearl and Cecil were kind and generous in their own way when I first moved in. Shortly after I arrived, Pearl offered to keep Sky for me and I accepted. As a massage therapist in a town with one stoplight, I had my work cut out just to drum up business. I did take Sky with me at first, but certain customers are put off, I feel, by the sight of a child. Particularly one as free in his nature as Sky is.

His stay at Pearl's house went well enough in the beginning. She respected the fact that Sky and I have chosen not to eat the dead flesh of animals and seemed content to ply him with such starch-and-sugar-filled concoctions as macaroni and cheese, pinto beans, and banana pudding, which I don't suppose hurt him in small quantities.

Pearl

She had that poor child eating as a vegerinarian. Of all things. I decided I'd best just not tell Ms. Starchild about that big old ham bone I always put to stewing in my pot along with the pintos Sky was eating up like they was the best thing he'd ever put in his mouth.

You'd think she might of figured it out when Sky took one of those ham bones and give it to that mangy old cur that had started hanging around, but she didn't. Why Sky's mother let him feed such animals is beyond me, but feed them he did, raccoons and possums, squirrels and chipmunks—any nasty old critter that came along. I say leave them to eat their own wild food and they're better off. But what does an old country woman know?

There is strange art in that house, too. There's a too big, cloudy white photograph in the living room of her feeding Sky—one fat white breast hanging out for all to see, the other side flat as a pancake. And the child looks old enough to walk in that picture. My own dear momma, God rest her soul, may have suckled all 11 of her children until they were walking and talking but I understand that she did not know any better and had circumstances. They did not have science back then like we have now. All four of *mine* were weaned from the bottle and toilet trained by the time they were one year old.

Sky

Mom and Miss Pearl got mad, but I didn't. I like them both.

Henna

Pearl kept Sky three mornings a week for me for almost a year. I paid her what I could, baked her homemade bread and offered my massage services free of charge in order to ease the symptoms of her gout. She declined. Still things proceeded well enough and Sky was happy to stay there. There was some mild strain between us after the oak tree lost a limb and damaged a portion of her roof. She seemed to believe I bore some responsibility for the course of nature.

The first Tuesday in June I came home to find them in the backyard laughing and sitting at the picnic table. I took a bench and joined them, worn out after a long day involving a stubborn rotator cuff and a patient with fibromyalgia who takes a holistic approach to muscle stimulation and requires an exhausting full-body massage.

As soon as I sat down Sky said, "Miss Pearl gave me pop!" in a voice thick with adoration.

"Pop?" I gave Pearl a questioning look.

"Sky's stomach was sour."

"I was green!" Sky yelled. "Green around my guilt!"

"Inside voice, Sky," I said. "And it's 'gills.'"

"We're outside," said Pearl.

"If by 'pop' you mean soda," I said, turning to her, "I don't allow him to have soda. I've told you that, Pearl."

"The boy was sick. I know a sour stomach when I see one."

"As do I, but my remedy uses wild ginger and works without the artificial stimulants of sugar and caffeine."

"Well, fine. That's fine. He only had a little anyway. And it was diet, so I don't reckon he got any sugar. The Tagamet's what really worked."

"Diet?" I said, my voice rising. "And Tagamet?"

To which she said, "Oh, for heaven's sake. There's no need to get all riled up. The doctor gave them to me for heartburn. I get it bad at night. No sooner do I lay down then up it comes. Tagamet's the only thing to work. Sky feels better. Don't you, boy?"

"I'll thank you to leave Sky out of this, Pearl. At five years old he does not know what is best for him. And besides, he is my child, not yours."

"Well I raised up four of my own and most of my ten brothers and sisters and have got eleven grandbabies. I think I know a thing or two about younguns."

"Well I am Sky's mother, and I do not want my son being exposed to drugs of any kind. I did not put one single artificial substance into my body during my pregnancy. I did not spray aerosol cans. I did not drink alcohol. Sky's system is not used to *drugs*."

"For your information, Tagamet is not a drug," she said. "It is a medicine."

"Well then you are practicing medicine without a license, and I should report you to the police."

With that, I pulled Sky up and dragged him home, an action I am not proud of, as I have always allowed him free will, but do it I did. And I did not approach Pearl after that.

Not, anyway, until the day of the accident.

Pearl

Judge not lest ye be judged, is what the Bible says, and I try hard to uphold that, but my high and mighty neighbor makes it hard. That poor child won't know what the world is like if his mother gets her way. I hate to think how he'll break out when he finally leaves home and realizes what all his momma has kept from him. Poor sheltered little thing, stuck playing with that scrawny half-wild dog they'd been feeding. You couldn't make me touch a sneaky looking stray like that with a ten-foot pole, nor would I let any child of mine near it, but you just try telling that to my neighbor, Miss All-nature-is-holy.

Sky

We fed Smoky. He was nice but he got mad. He barked. It felt like fire.

Henna

The terrible aspect of that incident that has lodged in my memory is the utter lack of sound. Perhaps the deadliest evil is always silent. I've seen that moment in my mind a thousand times since, and the same fact resurfaces as many times: I didn't realize anything was wrong. I saw it, and I stood there thinking Sky and Smoky were playing, roughhousing in a natural, animal way. Smoky had Sky down on the ground sort of rolling him around. I remember smiling; my own heart warmed to think of Sky reaching out to the soul of that unloved dog.

Pearl

It was the heebie jeebies down the back of my neck, like hackles on a hound that made me grab Cecil's .22. He wasn't walking right, that animal. He was skulking low and slow across the backyard while Sky stood there holding his hand out, thinking every creature in the world is kind. I'd of tore that hound away from Sky with my bare hands if I'd had to. I'd of give him my own throat to save Sky's.

Henna

I remember just having had the thought that I should go closer to check on Sky and Smoky when I saw Pearl running from her backyard to ours, carrying a big shotgun, or rifle or whatever. My first thought was that she would hurt Sky and I ran to the screen door and yelled, "Stop!"

I am not proud of that.

Pearl

I ran out back of my house to Sky and that dog not knowing I could move so fast. Out loud I thanked Cecil for keeping his .22 loaded and God for my legs. I prayed as I ran, "Help me Lord to save this child." I knew I'd have to shoot pointblank. There wasn't any choosing in it.

Henna

Sky needed me. I knew it then and felt his eyes cry out to me across the distance in a way his mouth could not. I shoved aside the screen door and ran onto the back porch in a frenzy of movement. I ran to the steps and grabbed the railing hard. And I froze. My body would not move. So I stood there. And watched.

Pearl

That nasty black thing had Sky pinned. I could feel pure evil coming off it in waves. I knew I didn't have time to wait for Cecil or Henna or nobody. I put that .22 straight to that demon's head. The bottom half of Sky's face and throat was in its jaws.

I prayed not to miss.

Henna

I watched from the porch: Pearl and Sky—my son with his eyes wild and staring up towards the house, his mouth so very wide open— and that dog holding Sky fast with a paw on his chest. I did not hear him growl. It looked to me, then, as if he were eating my child.

I suppose that image will remain with me forever.

Pearl

The gun went off with a muffled whump and the bullet sunk in the dirt. Praise God, that evil thing fell limp. I prized the devil's jaws apart and took Sky to his momma. He was breathing little fast short breaths, staring at everything and seeing nothing. His mouth was tore and his teeth and gums shone out in an awful red smile. There was so much blood.

Henna

I stood there and held my baby and stared. I soaked up his blood with my shirt. I lifted the flap of skin and pressed it back to his cheek. I cried. I remember Pearl saying, "Come on, girl. We got to go," and I must have followed. I don't remember. I'm told Pearl got ice and her keys and put us in her car and drove us to Montgomery Regional. She is said to have made the half-hour drive in 15 minutes.

Sky

I eat milkshakes every day. The stitchings itch and the stretches hurt. But Miss PT says I have to smile.

Pearl

I reckon I been forgiven for the tree. The Lord giveth and the Lord taketh away. At least He's given an old fool and a young fool and an innocent child another chance to make something out of love and life.

Henna

Each life experience is a lesson. The lesson will be repeated until we learn it. A child is not a tree. Not all creatures are good. Every person has hard-won wisdom, and a backcountry old woman *can* teach me things. If I'm respectful and accepting, I just might learn.

Sky

Miss Pearl told me a secret. She got mom a baby tree.

wholesale

There are memories better left fettered in the darkness, untended, unfed, growing long, leggy, and pale, but never finding fruition. They rise unbidden, these images, surfacing in the quiet moments between thoughts, in the darkest hour of the morning, in the stillness of the body, when the mind is wont to wander.

She came into this world impatient to get on with life. Small dark head of hair emerged restless from the womb, shoulders followed, and she pulled her arms free, pushing herself out like climbing up out of a pool. No need to slap this baby—her wail surrounded them in the bright white room—even the mother, through her stupor, heard her child's lungs unfolding for the first time.

Maggie Rand paces the front of the classroom. "Okay, here's your assignment, guys: I want you to give me five pages on forgiveness." The hands shoot up but she ignores them. "Any kind of forgiveness. Use your imagination. A rich guy forgiving a bum for stealing from him, a child forgiving abusive parents, an ex-prostitute forgiving herself. You decide."

"How about a professor forgiving a student for not getting the assignment done?" asks a voice from across the room.

"Sure," she says. "I'll accept fantasy."

In the bright chaos of daily life, the plain before me lies open, unobstructed. I teach, I modify, I understand. Yet darkness brings a frightful twisted bramble, a thorn-riddled maze with no shortcuts, and wretched rasping demons that lurk behind each dead end.

Soggy oats clumped and swayed in the sloshing bathwater as the child scratched at the blister-filled bumps covering her body. She scratched until they popped and oozed then sighed as the peaceful delirium of a well-scratched itch spread throughout her body. She had just begun to scratch a fat welt on her cheek when the father came in, clearing his throat loudly. He stared down at the child, sitting in the clotted water, hugging her knees to her chest. "Mags," he said, in a voice heavy with disapproval, "you've got to learn some self-control."

"I'm itchy," she said.

"Your mother and I have told you not to scratch, have we not?"

"It feels good to scratch."

"Scratching will give you an infection. It will make scars. It will make the chicken pox worse. You have to learn not to scratch."

"Daddy, I can't. My body likes it. Scratching makes my itches happy."

The father sighed and sat down beside the tub. "Give me your arm," he said. She glanced up at his face, then extended her forearm over the edge of the tub.

"See this bump?" When she nodded he took her by the wrist and said, "Watch." With his other hand he scratched in a circle around the blister, staying just outside the reach of angry redness.

"Scratching *around* the itch satisfies the craving, Mags, but doesn't hurt your body. It gives you time to heal. Got it?"

She nodded.

"But it doesn't feel as good," she said.

Maggie stands in the early morning line, on the seedy side of town, between a suited executive and a rasping, jittery, bag of bones. The line moves and they inch forward looking straight ahead, familiar in their plight, familiar by sight, yet none acknowledging the others.

Maggie has an hour, on Tuesday and Thursday, to get over here and back to campus before the start of her nine o'clock Comp Lit class. On Monday, Wednesday and Friday she hits the line later since her office hours begin at ten those days. On weekends she doesn't sleep in.

She stares at the familiar gray wall of the building before her, scrawled with a rash of graffiti kings' bright epithets to fame. The lot one-over contains a ramshackle house of peeling paint and broken shards of window through which a woman wearing a silver scarf watches the line advance. The acrid smell of urine stings Maggie's nostrils but she can't pinpoint the source. Perhaps it is the man behind her. Perhaps it is the doorway of a nearby apartment building. Perhaps it is the pervasive stench of desperation.

She feels a tug at her elbow and turns. The man behind her looks imploringly at her face. He must weigh all of 75 pounds. When she meets his gaze he smiles, revealing orange teeth with brown crevices between them and streaks of black rot inching downward from the gumline. His skin is leathery and creased. The skeletal gauntness of his frame and face make it impossible to judge his age.

"Got a smoke?" he asks.

You aren't supposed to panhandle in line and Maggie knows this, but she does have a cigarette. She's planning to quit, it's just impossible right now what with her packed course load, the ridiculous office hours she drew this semester, the unending piles of papers to grade, and coming here every morning for her daily dose of tolerance; her scratch *around* the itch.

She glances left and right then reaches into her jacket pocket, palms a cigarette and opens it behind her back. The man extricates the cigarette without touching her hand; he says nothing.

I want you to understand the whole tale. Wholesale. My soul sale. Somewhere, within the play of words I am safe. Therein lies my redemption. The right

combination will form a chain, and lead me to forgiveness, where absolution
waits beyond the door with no knob no window and no keyhole.

The father sat back on his distressed leather couch as the liquor rose and swirled like an oil slick in his cut glass tumbler. "Mags, I understand from the principal that you are smoking."

"Yeah?" she said, pinching up the fabric of her pants. "All the kids do. So?"

"Your mother found these in your jacket pocket." He held up a thin packet of rolling papers.

"Those aren't mine."

"Mags, are you doing drugs?"

"Those aren't mine. I don't even know what they're for."

"They're *for* rolling marijuana cigarettes. What are they doing in your jacket?"

"Jeez, Dad, they're not mine. I don't know. Why don't you trust me? You don't ever believe me."

"I will not have a daughter of mine using drugs. You got that?"

"Yeah," she said, looking away. "I got it."

"Jordan, your writing is very good," Maggie tells the student sitting across her desk for the mid-semester conference. "Edgy, but good." He stares at her blandly and smiles without his eyes, which appear to be all ice-blue irises. The pupils sit like tiny pinpricks in the vastness of them, unmistakable eyes of heroin. He's wearing a long-sleeved concert T-shirt advertising a band she doesn't know, with a gruesome picture of blood and gore.

Maggie stares at him for a moment, then tilts her head in the direction of a poster she has hung on her office wall with the poem "Invictus" printed on it. She recites the first stanza. "Out of the night that covers me / Black as the Pit from pole to pole / I thank whatever gods may be / For my unconquerable soul." The student looks at her with heavy-lidded eyes. "What do you think Henley is trying to say with those words, Jordan?"

He stares at the writing on the wall and moves his lips while reading silently. "Uh, I dunno," he says with a shrug. "Life is hell?"

She shifts forward in her seat, leaning closer. "I think he's saying that life *can* be hell. But also that our choices keep us there, or free us from it, according to our actions. Does that make sense to you?"

"Sure, I guess so," he says. "Shit happens."

"But we make the shit, Jordan. We are the instruments of our own destruction; likewise our redemption. Do you get it?"

"I get it," he says, edging away. "I get it."

So. You are to be my confidant? You will absolve me, I suppose. That's fair enough. But give me a moment. A moment yet to breathe as the woman others know. One moment to enjoy the construct of my life before the wrecking ball appears. A moment yet to salvage the few remaining precious bits I cannot bear to lose.

The 16-year-old woman-girl hitched the shoulder bag higher and stuck her thumb out into the oncoming traffic. By now she was miles from her parents' prying eyes. Waning sunlight warmed the backs of her bare legs and she squinted against the glinting grills of oncoming cars. Not one slowed down.

Sweat gathered under her breasts, pooling in the center and soaking the knot of her halter to a limp turquoise. The roots of her hair were damp and she pushed the #34 ash blond strands of it away from her face then dug into her bag for a pack of cigarettes. A smoke was what she needed.

Before she could find the pack, a blue Impala with a pimple-faced boy at the wheel slowed down and she threw her thumb back out. He leaned across the front seat and yelled, "Hey!" The passenger flinched and pushed him back to the driver's side, then stared back at her as they drove away. He held up a homemade Plexiglas bong with one hand and made the two-fingered *V* of a peace sign with the other. She watched the dust swirl and fade as the Impala pealed off. Shit. She could've used a hit. If only her parents hadn't found her stash and fucking flushed it she'd have had a fat joint snuggled inside that wad of bills she took.

She switched thumbs and gritted a smile then turned and walked backward, squinting into the furiously setting sun. She should have brought her sunglasses. But what the hell. You can't be expected to remember everything when you're packing for the rest of your life.

Maggie stares hard at the locked door trying to fix it into place but it shudders and clatters before her eyes. So cold. So fucking cold. No one said she'd be so fucking cold. She reaches an arm out from under the blankets and stares at the rash of small bumps that rise like a wave down her arm, lifting the small hairs. Her arm is foreign. It is the fresh plucked skin of cold turkey flesh. It is hideous.

She pulls her arm back under the weight of blankets and stills the image. The arm aches as if beaten with a club. Twenty hours and *all* of her aches. She must not let her mind consider how to stem this agony, crossing instead her wrists over her abdomen just before the next wave of gooseflesh turns to nausea and she is retching in the trash can wishing it were that simple and could be but thrown up, thrown out, thrown away.

Desire lives within me, breathing with my breath, feeding on itself, constant as a pulse, inevitable as heartbeats, insistent as a sore that will not heal. I dream of chasing my protector, begging for his warmth and peace. Then he turns and chases me, wielding peace and warmth to slip to me against my will. I cry out, "Stop!" But always he succeeds. Always, I am the one who finds the vein.

She felt good. The drinks were free. Nobody treated her like a kid. The tokes were free and she was beautiful. Everybody wanted her. Beautiful and burning free. Free as flying. Flying on shiny wings of life as high as life could be. She stared at the liquid man in his radiant coffee-colored skin.

"It's a cocktail," he said.

"Like a drink?"

"No," he said, flashing an ivory smile. "A speedball."

"A speedball." She looked into his eyes. The shining jet-black iridescent holes sucked at her until she stumbled and fell. He picked her up. "What does it do?"

"Do? Baby, it makes you king. It speeds up life. You rule the world."

"Antoine," a far-off voice said, "don't *kill* her, man, she's a kid."

She grabbed his arm and pulled him to her hard. "I want to fly," she said, and she could feel it in her eyes.

But when he brought the needle, a black crow beat its wings inside her chest, screeching and clawing to get out, out. He held her wrist and she thought to scream but as it rose up in her she saw the needle sliding gently under her skin and a small blister rose up as if to explode. She held her arm out, watching the bubble even as he withdrew the needle tip and pulled her to him, cradling her head in the crook of his arm.

"Shh," he said although she hadn't made a sound. She stared over his elbow at the bubble on her outstretched forearm. It flattened and began to disappear. "Shh, baby," he said. "Take it in easy, just a skin pop. No vein, baby, no vein."

The last of the bubble faded to a small white circle and there was a rising surge in her belly that swelled and spread out warm, buttery, love flowing over her chest, her arms, her legs, into her fingertips and toes and her scalp glowed and she was held up, cradled, embraced by giant arms that would never let her fall.

"I've tried it on my own. I just can't do it, you know?" Maggie crosses and uncrosses her legs. "I mean, the methadone works, as long as those Gestapo clowns don't try to ease me off like they think I won't notice. Who tells them to do that? I'm on maintenance, right? Maintenance. Status quo and all that. Why do they think they can screw with that? It's still my body, right?"

"Yes, Maggie, it's still your body. I think you know that," the counselor says.

"Last time I checked, but I mean who gave them the right?"

"You're upset. I understand," he says behind steepled fingers.

"You understand?" She lifts an eyebrow.

"Come now, Maggie, I see more than you know."

Her response is a snort.

"You disagree?"

"Yeah, I disagree." She jogs her foot up and down. "You see the pitiful human shells that thirst and burn, but you haven't lived it. You haven't felt that surge of lava rolling through your heart, that peace and warmth you never want to quench, that love that slowly dies within you, freezes you out until you add more and more but still it dims and dulls and leaves you lizard cold." She smiles. "Sorry Doc. You haven't seen shit."

He sighs. "Maggie, I am not the enemy. I'm trying to help you here."

"So help me," she says, running fingers through her hair. "Tell the clowns to quit messing with my dosage."

He looks at her for a long moment. "I authorized that," he says. "Your urine came back dirty."

"Yeah? And Carlos told me his came back pregnant."

"I'm not at liberty to discuss other patients."

"Look, I know you think he switched urine on you. God knows how, when your fetishistic goons stand over us and watch us eke it out."

"Maggie, you know full well that without systems in place—"

"Fuck your systems. What about our dignity?"

"Look, Maggie. If you care to—"

"Oh, I care. And for the record, my urine wasn't dirty until you docked my dosage. I need the methadone. The full amount."

"Our therapy is designed to be temporary. You know that."

"I know this: I used for ten years, Doc. Ten years. And six months doesn't make a dent in that. And your fucking syrupy orange handcuffs drive my life. You think I like coming down here every day to stand in line and relive how I screwed up over and over again? You think I like pissing in a cup while some clown with a tenth grade education breathes down my neck? You think I like that? You ever try it?"

"Look, Maggie, you need—"

"I *need* methadone. As nasty as the shit is, it lets me live my life. I've tried coming off it on my own. I can't." She takes a deep breath. "I can't."

"Listen Maggie, the only thing you can't do is throw away the crutch before you've learned to walk. I want to see you get your life back as much as you do, but first you've got to get over this anger of yours. I think we need to look into some relaxation therapy for you."

"Relaxation? Tell you what, Doc. You try sitting on a keg of dynamite holding a blowtorch—we'll see how relaxed you feel."

I drift through a graveyard of abandoned emotions, visiting by turns the sad stone markers—monuments to the depths a soul can slide. To my left lies the wily Wantonness of youth, the greatest loss, the first to go. To the right, the fitful resting place of Shame, banished years earlier, doggedly slow to die. Another plot enfolds the twins, inseparable in death as in life: Craving and Cowardice here lie entwined, rejoined to oneness in the slow rot of ruin. And last, beneath this crimson mound, a deadly defiant Anger dwells. Killed with my bare hands, it has risen, tormented from the grave, stronger in its afterlife.

She applied the makeup carefully, each stroke a meditation, a prayer. The ashen geisha face peered pleading from the mirror, lips drawn beyond their boundaries in brown pencil, gaps filled by a slick of purple to trick the eye. She opted for Cleopatra eyes, dark with charcoal, rimmed in pouty soot. Studying her reflection, it struck her that the effect was one of violent aftermath: a sickly pallor underlying swollen purple lips and slightly sunken eyes already beginning to bruise.

She held the smooth cool cylinder up to the light and tested the plunger, then looked past it and spoke to her reflection.

"One more time," she said as a silver bead rose from the tip of the needle and slid slowly down its length.

"Just one more."

"Jordan, will you stay after for a moment?" Maggie asks as the students file past at the end of Creative Writing.

"Yeah?" he says. "What?" His eyes fix on a spot above her head. They are tiny pinpricks. "Pinned" she used to say. She stares at this kid with a mixture of sympathy and collusion. Another initiate into the club. She thinks of the '80's roach motel slogan: *They check in, but they don't check out.*

"I may be overstepping my bounds here Jordan, but I—"

"Then don't."

"I think you might need some help."

"I don't."

"Jordan," she says moving closer, "are you on heroin?"

"No." He steps back. "Jesus. You're not my mom."

"Maybe not, Jordan, but you've got to know. Someone's got to tell you." She takes another step towards him. "*I've* got to tell you."

He stares at her, blinking rapidly and breathing in short little gasps. "No you don't," he says. "Really. I'm good. I swear."

"Jordan." She puts a hand on his arm. "Heroin feels like your friend at first. It feels like love. But in the end you're just left holding the bag. You chase that first time over and over again, trying to recreate it, but you can't, Jordan. You never find that first love again. It's a hideous lie. It's not your friend."

"Um, yeah." He steps back and shrugs off her hand. "Sure." He picks at a blemish on his chin and looks around her office. "Uh, no offense or anything, but what the hell would you know about it?"

Triggers, they say. Beware them.
Like Pavlov's dogs I drool
for wads of money,
for loneliness,
for knowing it is there.

no reason not to

S he's got good days and bad days.
Sometimes the days pass right quick-like, and she'll go for hours, pushing it down and forgetting. But eventually the thoughts slip back in, centipede-like, through a crack in her concentration. Then that bright pain hits inside her head, lighting it up like a lava lamp, and she has to shake it hard to make the pain stop. That helps some. Like looking away when the needle goes into your arm to give blood. Actually, Eileen feels as if she's giving blood, or more that it's being taken from her—drip, drip, drip—draining away her life. She imagines her body when it's all over, skittering around the floor like used tissue paper.

Even sitting here, her favorite time of day, with Oprah spilling her sweet, smooth voice all over her guest like honey, Eileen can't make her head quit.

Sometimes it's Louetta Weeks. Lionel took Louetta to the senior prom. They were voted class couple. Fifteen years wasn't too long for something like that to resurface, come bobbing back up like a corpse in a flood.

Sometimes it's that new blonde, Tracy, in Lionel's office. Eileen remembers how he sort of shoved them together at the office picnic, saying how much they had in common. Like him? He'd enjoy almost getting caught, watching them sniff and search, and come up short at every dead end. Does Eileen suspect? Will Tracy blow his cover? Which path leads to the cheese?

Eileen knows what women think about. She knows Tracy watched her with the sharp eye of the other woman, thinking, *so that's Lionel's wife, no wonder he comes to me.* Sizing Eileen up. Tch-tching over her dull brown hair, I-see-now-ing over her three children. They clamor for Eileen's attention, tugging at her pants leg, tap, tap, tapping on her arm. And the other woman thinks *why does he stay with her?* And the baby cries blindly in the front pack, flailing his arms, while Eileen jiggles her body up and down, up and down, extending her hand, smiling. Nice to meet you.

These images keep Eileen awake at night. The one thing she never wanted to be was a fool. But there you go.

Lionel spent two weeks last summer on reserve duty in Panama. Maybe an exotic foreign hooker stopped him on the street. Gave him her business card from the brothel. Lured him with her long black hair, olive skin, red lips. Took him to a room in a local boarding house where she turned her tricks. It would have to be clean. Lionel might be unfaithful, but not in a dirty room. His momma taught him better than that.

She wonders if they kissed.

Or was it when he got sent to Saudi for the Gulf War? Maybe a Brit, with a sexy name like Sam, who whispered her accented dirty words in his ear when they did it. *Oh yes, Luv. Quite right. That's the ticket.* In bed they would call each other Sergeant and snuggle together, with knowing, throaty chuckles. "My wife," he would say, not using her name, "has fat thighs." And they'd laugh together. The ultimate betrayal.

Dixianna was three when Lionel was called up. Eileen hugged him good-bye over the huge mound of her belly while the baby kicked at him through the thin blanket of flesh. Mindy came early. Three weeks sooner than she was supposed to, two weeks after Lionel shipped out. So Tammy ended up in the delivery room with Eileen, holding her hand and praying while Baby Mindy squeezed herself out into the world.

Tammy's husband Joe drilled with Lionel's unit, but Joe wasn't called up, on account of his back, so Tammy helped Eileen when she could. They organized a Christmas cookie brigade from Floyd Baptist Church so the boys overseas could have home-cooked goodies. They put up a hundred yellow ribbons till the sight of them made her sick. She wrote Lionel a letter every day to keep up his spirits. Morale was a sensitive thing and Eileen didn't want to be the cause of him coming home all shattered and out of place like those Vietnam vets did.

She doesn't remember that war, of course, except for summer trips to the beach with her family, passing trucks full of soldiers going down Interstate 64. For the big rigs she made a fist up, honk-your-horn sign, and for the soldier trucks a two-fingered peace sign. The truckers always honked, and the soldiers always answered her peace signs with their own. If she closes her eyes, she can still see them, hanging out the back of the trucks, grinning—green canvas flapping around behind them, hot asphalt slipping away beneath them. She thinks about them now, dying with a little girl's peace sign in their heads.

"I'm not a writer," is what Lionel said, but he did call from Saudi when he felt lonely. It was usually three a.m. in Virginia when the phone rang and the panic rose up in Eileen's throat so she could hardly say hello. She was always certain it was The Call, but then there Lionel would be on the other end, laughing at her worry.

Usually he wanted her to talk dirty, wanted to get excited long distance. "Tell me what you're wearing," he'd say, with the echo of a pause as his voice bounced across the moon. Groggy and crabby, with the baby starting to wake, she'd struggle to find something to say, reach down deep to think of something that would get him going.

Eileen never could confront Lionel over the phone. She couldn't handle the long, expensive silences that went nowhere. Actually, she doesn't think she can confront him now, either. Maybe she just can't deal with it. Anyway, she has to *think*.

Of course, thinking is about all she's been able to do lately, and she finds herself doing stupid stuff like putting the fork in the trash and the napkin in the dishwater. Even Oprah can't bring Eileen out of her funk today. She's had the TV on for most of the show, trying to get uplifted, since Oprah promised her shows would be inspirational from here on out. But the show is about living with AIDS. Try as she might, Eileen just can't get uplifted thinking about living with AIDS.

Eileen finished high school. She was class valedictorian, which ought to count for something. She isn't dumb, but she can't account for the way things have turned out. Before all these kids she used to be a working woman. If Lionel hadn't swept her off her feet, she'd probably be manager at the Kroger's in Christiansburg by now.

Lionel was so charming back when they were dating. He used to show up at Kroger's the days she had to work late, and she'd see him at the back of the line, whistling, not looking at her. Then when he'd get up to the register he'd have some fancy cheese and crackers from the gourmet section, and a six pack of those wine coolers that were just getting popular. It was his secret message to her. Or he might buy a red rose and some fancy foreign chocolate. Lionel knew she'd get to thinking, and he was right. She'd get all hot under her apron. One time he bought a bottle of baby oil and a cucumber. She'd spent the rest of her shift blushing and fretting. She always did, though. If a lady bought sanitary pads or a pregnancy test, or a man bought hair color or Preparation H, she couldn't look them in the eye when she told them their total.

Eileen can't figure how things got this way with her and Lionel. Did she get to the point where she liked being taken for granted? Maybe she got satisfaction out of being The Woman With The Most Inconsiderate Husband, saving up stories until she could top the best of them. Like her 30th birthday when Lionel kept the kids and sent Eileen all the way out to Hooters in Roanoke with the other realtors and secretaries from his office. She was pregnant with Lionel Junior at the time, and big as a house, in no mood to party. Half the people there didn't even know her name. The waitresses, in their cropped shirts and short shorts, bounced to the table with a piece of cake and sang and she was 30 and these strangers stared and clapped and told her to make a wish and asked her was Lionel coming and she chewed and smiled and tried to pretend that this was normal and okay with her, too polite to name a skunk. She drove home afterward with a sick pit in her stomach, parked the car with the lights off, sneaked out back behind the lilac bushes and vomited. Then she walked in to see Lionel's eager face, first thing, so pleased with himself. He wanted to hear every detail of her fun evening. Then he wanted sex.

Lionel had never been what you'd call sensitive, but Eileen couldn't have predicted his unfaithfulness. He was her husband. He said he loved her. She believed him. She had no reason not to.

She remembers the time early in the marriage, right after Dixianna's birth, when her Pap smear showed chlamydia, and she was called into the clinic for a private consultation. She thought it was a fancy word for a yeast infection, and just stared at the technician when he told her it was a sexually transmitted disease and no, you couldn't get it from a toilet seat. In a daze, she drove to her sister's to pick up Dixianna, her breasts leaking milk in big, wet circles on the front of her dress. Then she was so distracted she forgot to feed the baby and she had to stop right there on 221 at a Dumpster and nurse just to quiet her down. When Eileen got home and called Lionel at the sales office, she cried and told him she had an S.T.D., and it was shameful, that's what it was.

But Lionel put on his calm, patient voice and explained it all away. *Left over from our single days . . . false positives . . . what would it hurt to take the medicine, just in case?* He was so sweet and understanding. He said he didn't even suspect Eileen of being with another man, he trusted her that much.

Stupid now. Stupid! Stupid! Stupid! Was this always the way? You toss away the obvious until suddenly it hits you like a ton of bricks that you've been blind, deaf, and dumb? And at risk. This is the 90's and Eileen has watched enough TV to know that she could die from what Lionel might bring home to her.

Faithful. Trusting. Stupid. Dead.

She glances at the TV and there's a guest from Oprah's audience standing up at the microphone. She says she's a nurse who works with newborns who have AIDS. The nurse says they still don't know if HIV can travel through breastmilk or not, so if a mother thinks she could be infected she shouldn't breastfeed. Eileen can't breathe when she hears that. She has to do something. She has to protect herself, her family.

She finds the bottles of formula from the hospital, pre-mixed, on the back shelf of the pantry. Then she opens drawer after drawer in the kitchen, pushing junk aside, looking for the nipples. Where could they be? Why was she saving so many twist ties? And how many fast food straws did she really need anyway? Trouble was, you just never knew when those things might come in handy. And as sure as she threw something out, then she needed it the very next day. Hadn't Mindy needed that extra wire for her fairy wings? And actually, Eileen kept meaning to string Hawaiian leis with the kids using those straws like she saw in Family Circle's craft section last month. Maybe even have a family luau.

Finally, there's the nipple. She thinks she should sterilize it or something; but really, there isn't time if she's going to save the baby. So she screws it on and puts it quick in the baby's mouth. He sputters and chokes, and bites on the damn thing like he doesn't know what it's for. She tries again and again, pushing it farther in, until he's bawling and retching, and she's crying, "Here. Take it. Take it!" over and over, but it's no use.

Eileen pulls it out of the baby's mouth. His face is all red-purple from crying and his little fists are clenched, flailing at everything and nothing. Eileen is shocked by what she's done. She throws the bottle in the trash, nipple and all, and gives the baby her breast, sobbing and breathing in big gulps of air. He gets real still then and pauses mid-suck, staring at her, big-eyed, over the white mound of her breast.

Eileen knows what she must do, but the tasks ahead of her seem unbearable. More humiliating tests requested with a rushed explanation. Condoms. (Law, that's embarrassing.) Confronting her husband. Deciding whether she can live with him, looking at his lying face for the rest of her life.

The rest of her life.

Even if he says he'll give the other woman up, can she trust him? Eileen sees herself checking pockets, listening in on phone calls, calling hotel rooms late at night. She doesn't want to be that woman, but she can feel a tendrilled mass growing inside her already. Malignant. A tumor of distrust.

When Oprah goes off, Eileen decides to call Tammy, who's been through this with Joe twice before. All Tammy says is how the Good Lord meant for us to be forgiving and after she and Joe worked things out it made her love him even more. Eileen makes sympathetic noises over the phone, but hangs up as soon as she can. Secretly she thinks Joe is a jerk and Tammy is a fool, and vows not to call her again anytime soon. Joe got that 17-year-old waitress pregnant, for pity's sake. Thank goodness the girl decided to have an abortion, now at least they only have to see her every Sunday after church when they eat at the Waffle House on the bypass. That's punishment enough for Tammy. She could think of worse for Joe, though.

Then, since Eileen really doesn't know about anything anymore, she imagines Lionel in the same predicament. What if he has an illegitimate child somewhere? She lets the magnitude of that sink in slowly, wallowing in the possibilities, the future scenarios, the confrontations. Then the TV lights up all on its own and there's Sally Jesse Raphael smiling conspiratorially and saying, "Well, Eileen, I think you have a right to be angry," while the audience applauds. A baby's picture flashes on the stage monitor. "Lionel's baby by Crystal" captions the photo. The audience boos and hisses Lionel in his plush red chair, Eileen on his left, girlfriend Crystal on his right.

And Eileen's mother is the surprise guest on the show. She strides out from backstage, yelling, "Faithless bastard! Infidel!"

Somehow, these images are painful and comforting at the same time. Eileen is learning to let them flash through her brain until they are gone. She's decided to go with it. Work through it. Ride the wave. It's as if she's on an amusement park ride, like the one at Lakeside she rode as a child. Cloud Nine. They strap you in and you spin and spin until you can't even lift your arm or leg—a giant one of those things that spin your blood. Only she realizes too late that the attendant forgot to strap her in, and little pieces of her are flying off in every direction. She can't stop them and she can't get them back.

As a kid, Eileen would always imagine the worst possible scenario and make herself a plan. When she was eight, her parents took her to Virginia Beach. She held onto her daddy's hand and walked the long pier out into the ocean. When she looked down through the wooden planks at her feet, she saw the waves below, rolling toward the beach, and Eileen knew with a child's certainty that she would either slip through a crack or the whole pier would give way, leaving her to grab the biggest plank and hang on for dear life. So as she walked, she planned out in her head exactly what she would do, which plank she would go for.

When they drove over the Chesapeake Bay Bridge, her sister Debi tried to hold her breath the whole way, but Eileen carefully planned how she would escape the sinking car after a big truck ran them off the bridge.

The baby has fallen asleep at the breast. She tries to dislodge his lips without waking him, but he shifts around and opens his eyes. When he looks up at her so trusting, Eileen has a moment of panic. He starts to squirm and she makes a quick decision. She'll give him ice cream. It's made from milk. All kids like ice cream.

He shrieks when she tries to set him down, so she shifts him to the other hip, puts two spoons in her mouth, grabs the carton with her free hand, and heads for the table.

Eileen is just hooking the straps on the high chair when Lionel comes in with Dixianna and Mindy. He says Eileen had better get her shit together. Wouldn't he like to sit around all day eating ice cream? Maybe Eileen would like to go to work and support him for a change?

Over the buzzing in her head Eileen offers to fix him a bowl, but no, he has to go back by the office. He can't stay.

"Can you drop the kids by Momma's on your way out, then?" Eileen asks. "She's gonna sit them so I can get some housework done."

"I'm not driving. Wes is picking me up in five minutes." Lionel is suddenly charming, chucking the baby under the chin, smiling, kissing Eileen on the top of her head.

Grateful for the kindness, she overlooks the fact that Wes has three ex-wives, a big black Harley, and a drinking problem. He's been with Buffalo Realty about a month now, and he and Lionel have become best buddies. She's pretty sure Wes made a pass at her the first time they met.

"Can I have your keys then?" she asks as she offers the baby her spoon with just a dab of ice cream on the end. "The Plymouth won't start again." Lionel drops the keys into her lap with an exaggerated sigh, and she's sure the car would start if only she were smarter, thinner, better looking.

The baby sucks on the end of Eileen's spoon, gives her a toothless grin and smacks his lips for more. He opens wide like a baby bird and Eileen spoons in a whole bite. Shocked by the cold, he holds his mouth open, makes a panicky noise in his throat, and shakes his head back and forth. He won't spit it out though, because it tastes too good. Eileen laughs out loud and gives him another spoonful. Then Lionel starts laughing, which brings Dixianna and Mindy in to see what's so funny, and pretty soon everyone is laughing.

The baby loves being the center of attention and keeps on being silly until the whole family is laughing wide open, gasping for breath, and Eileen cries, "Oh my God, stop. Stop!"

In the middle of it all, the phone rings. Eileen answers it with the laughter still in her voice, breathless. "Hello?"

"Hello?" a woman's voice says in return.

"Yes. Hello." Eileen chuckles, mugging for Lionel as he pantomimes the baby's silly face for her, and she gasps, trying not to laugh, and thinks *this is it*. This is family at its best. They were still a family. No other woman could give him this. She sees it clearly in that frozen moment with her ear to the phone, Lionel ushering the girls upstairs, blowing Eileen a smiling kiss over his shoulder as he leaves through the front door.

"Hello?" says the woman again as if she can't hear. "Hello?"

So Eileen says it slowly, "Hell-lo," and the woman hangs up.

Connections are bad sometimes. Eileen knows this as well as anybody. It just seems odd that Eileen's end was so clear, and that woman couldn't hear. If it's important she'll call back.

Sure enough, not a minute later, the phone rings.

Lionel runs back in. "Forgot my wallet," he says with a grin, taking the steps two at a time, bounding up them while Eileen watches him and lets the phone ring an extra two times even though she's standing right there with her hand on the receiver.

"Hello," Eileen says. She makes it a statement not a question, and she's getting a bit annoyed. The floor needs mopping, after all. She doesn't feel like talking to anyone.

Lionel has grabbed the upstairs phone before her and his voice echoes too loudly in her ear, "Eileen, it's me. They hung up— wrong number or something. Anyway, I'm gone, Baby, okay?"

"Yeah, sure," she says, distracted, then hangs up and waits for the third call.

When it comes, Eileen puts her hand on the receiver and says out loud to no one, "Answering the telephone—take three," then lifts it up, pauses an extra moment and says, "Hello?"

It's her again. After a long moment the voice says, "Is this Eileen Quesenberry?" The words are slow and deliberate.

"Yes it is . . ."

Another long pause. "And are you married to Lionel Quesenberry?"

". . .Yes I am."

Eileen thinks it could still be a salesperson. *Please be a salesperson.*

"All right, then," says the woman, pronouncing each word distinctly, not running them together the way anyone from Floyd would.

The click of the receiver seems slow and deliberate, too, and Eileen stands there with the receiver to her ear, listening without breathing, hoping to find some clue in the stillness. She listens as hard as she can, willing the woman to come back on and be an old friend looking for Lionel, or a salesperson, or even a collection agency. She listens until there's only an insistent beep, beep, beep, echoing in her ear and she could just scream.

The baby starts to fuss and squirm in his high chair so she puts the whole carton of ice cream on his tray and sticks two spoons deep into it. Let him play with that. She needs to think.

That woman's voice, her words, her deliberateness. Eileen keeps trying to replay the calls in her mind, remember every word, dissect every nuance, but she's winded, knocked off her feet, nothing to grab hold of, nothing to stand on, no air to breathe. All she really wants is some security, some surety, some steady love. Even the ability to admit to the inability to stay faithful would be something. The honesty might actually be refreshing. Perhaps she would smile and throw her arms around Lionel if he finally admitted to being a thoughtless, faithless jerk.

Instead of confessing, though, he always pulls out some explanation that sounds so logical. Or even better, he offers none, and pretends to be just as baffled as Eileen by the whole thing. That's really clever.

The more Eileen thinks, the more she's certain what the phone calls were about, and the madder she gets until there's this great burning anger inside her. If she raised her shirt, she'd see it glowing, illuminating her from within, her bellybutton a dark circle against the glowing, pulsing radiation of her anger, her hurt, her fury.

Lionel must thank his lucky stars every night. He got a woman without a brain. Does he think she doesn't know? Oh, she could cut his thing off like that Bobbitt woman did and not even look back. Forget running down the street with it, she'd just flush the damn thing and be done with it. She wouldn't want somebody putting it in a cup of ice and sewing it back on later.

Although, a Velcro attachment would be good. That way,

whenever he left the house, she'd just say, "Oh Honey, you forgot again," with a big toothy grin and then *scriiick*, off it'd come, and she'd lay it out in a cigar box until he got home. A big, fat stogie and she'd be in charge of it for a change. Teach it some manners.

Eileen's stomach is boiling. She's absolutely starving. She'll never get anything done on an empty stomach. Cheesecake. That's what she needs. Cheesecake to dull the ache, blanket the agony. The thought's hardly registered before she's in the kitchen dragging out the Sara Lee box. It doesn't even matter that it's frozen. Eileen attacks it with the fork, stabbing into each bite, launching it into her mouth rapid-fire. Her cheeks are bulging, and each swallow is really more of a contained choke, but things won't get better until she sees the bottom of the box.

She uses the flat side of the fork after the cake is mostly gone, smashing the remaining crumbs through the tines, bringing them to her lips, greasy from the crust and the cake and the fury of it all. On the last bite she chews and chews until it's mush. Still she chews, making up for all she swallowed whole.

Hanging on the wall in front of her is this Serenity Prayer her momma cross-stitched for her. *God, grant me the serenity to accept the things I cannot change, the courage to blah, blah, blah.* As Eileen reads it, she's staring at it, licking her finger and pressing it into the crumbs, thinking, *God, grant me the serenity to eat the things I cannot change . . .*

The girls are at the door, coats on, fighting. The baby has ice cream everywhere. Eileen told her momma she'd have the kids there by 5:30 and it's after that already. Cleaning is out of the question, unless it's the mess of her life she can mop up, spray off, dust away. Instead she grabs the ice cream baby, pulls his shirt off, and turns on the tap while he fiddles with the sprayer. As Eileen grabs a dishrag the phone rings and she reaches for it, one arm towards the phone one arm towards the baby. She's pretty sure who it is this time so she says, "I'm on my way, Momma," and sets the receiver back in its cradle.

While she's wiping his face, the baby figures out the sprayer and shoots a long arc of water down the front of Eileen's shirt, then squirts himself in the eye and starts crying. She pronounces him clean enough, throws him into a diaper, and puts on his little red sleep suit and coat. She gives the girls the rest of a bag of cheese puffs to stop them from bickering, then loads everyone into Lionel's truck and heads off to her momma's house.

It's early, but the winter sun is long gone, dropped behind a mountain, shrouding route 221 in eerie twilight. Eileen tries first her high beams, then her low, but nothing cuts through the strange half-light. Dixianna and Mindy fight over the cheese puffs, yanking the bag back and forth with loud crumpling sounds. The truck fills with noise. Eileen reaches over and turns on the radio to drown them out while the baby wipes orange fingers on his car seat. She starts to yell at him, but decides she has enough on her mind anyway, what with this stinking truck and its impossible gear shift that only Lionel can work without grinding and Lord she'll be lucky if she doesn't wreck the thing.

That's about the time Eileen rounds the big curve at El Tenador, the old skating rink, and sees the deer, but doesn't see it, too. As in, *oh, a deer. Isn't that nice.* The buck ambles across the road and Eileen's headlights catch him halfway across. He stands there, transfixed, frozen in the headlights. Eileen keeps driving, frozen in her thoughts. She tries to count the points of his antlers the way Lionel taught her back when they were dating and she pretended to like hunting just to be around him. Ten points? Twelve? She sees his haunches quiver as he stands there mesmerized, like in some part of his brain he knows he should run away, but can't make his muscles work. Eileen is just deciding that she is The Deer in the Headlights, imagining the thud of his magnificent body against the fender, when Mindy screams, spewing orange spit everywhere.

Eileen yanks the wheel hard, hits a patch of gravel on the side of the road, and does a 180. The deer bounds away while the road dust dances in her headlights. The baby claps his hands and Mindy sobs while Eileen tries to make her shaking hands work the gearshift.

She drops the kids off at her momma's without getting out of the truck. Dixianna carries the baby. Eileen's momma stands in the doorway, silhouetted by the porch light. Her breath puffs out indignantly into the night air, casting its own long, disapproving shadow. Eileen lets the truck idle at the end of the driveway until she sees the kids safely inside.

She backs out, accidentally spraying gravel from the unfamiliar clutch, and heads back to the main road then turns onto the Parkway. The Blue Ridge Mountains could always clear her head. She drives to a scenic overlook and parks.

She could leave Lionel. But in such a small town she'd never really get away. She could make him jealous, hurt him like he hurt her, but that wasn't really her style and anyway, who would want a Mother of Three? She could take a Greyhound bus to Charlotte, or New Orleans, or Tampa, and start a new life. That was tempting. But there were the kids to think about. She could pray for Lionel to change—Tammy's solution. Or she could simply wait it out; she'd already been doing that for 10 years.

Eileen sits and stares at the lights in the valley below. They pulse and throb and beckon to her. Who would miss her if she were just to drive right off the edge of this big old mountain? It seems like an easy solution. So very, very easy. And restful. Except Eileen begins to picture the car flipping over and over, then devises a plan in her head for surviving the crash. Her mind interferes even in this.

When she realizes her fingertips and nose have gotten numb sitting in the cold, she starts the engine and heads back toward town. She pulls onto 221 near the sign that says Ray's Rest. (The sign maker had run out of room, but it was more of a bar than a restaurant anyway.) Eileen slows to check out the parking lot. Just as she is almost past, she pulls into the lot, surprising herself. She sits in the truck until she musters enough of her new go-with-it attitude, gets out, and slams the door.

Then she stands there, suddenly indecisive. As she reaches for the handle to climb back into the truck, she hears her name called.

"Hey, Eileen! Ain't seen you around lately. Where you been keeping yourself? You coming in?"

"Why Daryl Agnew," she yells across the lot. "I wouldn't miss the chance to play catch-up over a redeye. How's that wife of yours?"

"Afraid you'll have to ask my lawyer."

"Well, now, that's a shame. You just give me a second. I'll be there directly." Eileen slips off her wedding band and holds it in the palm of her hand, feeling the warmth of the gold. She hasn't taken it off once since the day Lionel slipped it on her finger 10 years back. For effect she lets it fall through the air into the coat pocket she holds open with her other hand. There's something satisfying in the extra flourish, and she pats the outside of the pocket for good measure.

Once inside, Eileen sits on a barstool next to Daryl. Ray gives her a nod. "Redeye?" he says, gesturing with the glass.

When she nods he pours a shot of tomato juice into a glass mug, then holds the mug on a slant at the tap, and the beer slides into the tomato juice, making a faintly orange head of foam. He slips a napkin under the bottom of the mug and sets it in front of her.

As Eileen reaches for her redeye she stares at the white place on her finger. It looks obscene, like a dead fish belly, and she thrusts her hand into her pocket. She locates the ring and slips it on awkwardly with her thumb and pinkie.

When she grabs her mug, it clinks against the glass.

evangeline

My momma, she named me Evangeline. I reckon she was trying to make me a Christian before I ever even drew my first breath. She figured giving me a name like that, I couldn't help but turn out right. Poor Momma. If raising me up taught her one thing, it taught her you can't throw a good name on something bad and have it come up smelling sweet. Everybody must've thought Cain was a right smart name for a baby boy, too, till he grew up and killed his brother.

And even though a body might call his self a *Sanitation Engineer*, he still spends all day picking up smelly old bags of coffee grounds, rotten fruit, and dirty diapers. So I don't hold much to naming a thing for the hope you stick on it. I figure old Romeo hit pretty close to the bone when he said a rose by any other name would smell as sweet. Well I'm here to tell you, it's the same with shit.

I done my best. I was in church every time they cracked the door. Can I help it if my favorite Bible book turned out to be Song of Solomon? All that talk about lips of wine and feeling it in the bowels. I can relate to that stuff.

Of course, by the time all the trouble started, I was calling myself Eve, and Momma figured I was the original sinner.

Only, I weren't. Cause all of us is sinners, and all of us is bad. Can't nobody live up to the Lord. Not even Momma. Granny says

Momma got her religion the day she birthed me. I got born, and Momma got Born Again. Of course, having a baby at 15 would make anybody act crazy, especially if you didn't know where the baby's daddy had got to.

I was named for my daddy—for his job, anyways. Granny says he was an evangelical preacher, and traveled around spreading God's word and bringing lost souls to Jesus. What I can't picture is Momma getting all wrought up over some traveling preacher and making a baby like that. He weren't here long—stayed for a week of revival, then lit out of town.

And that's all I know. It ain't as if Granny likes talking about the shame of her life—her only baby girl in a family way like that, and no husband. I bet it like to killed her. Paw Paw was deacon of Holy Rock of Jesus Church at the time, but he stepped down when everybody found out what Momma had done.

I imagine me a daddy who's young and handsome, dark-headed and dark-eyed, and sorty skinny-like. A tall drink of water. I know I favor him. I sure don't take after nobody in this family. Sometimes I'll catch Momma looking at me so hard she'll about stare a hole in me, and then I know I'm a living reminder of her sin that won't never go away.

The whole county knows my story. It ain't no big secret. In grade school everybody called me Vangie and I had me plenty of friends. But at Stonewall Jackson High, everything turned different. The girls whispered and looked away. The boys made jokes and laughed real loud. I figured I had some past to live up to—a preacher's daughter *and* a bastard.

I kept waiting for things to get better. They never did. The summer before 10th grade I quit the stupid school and ran away. I got a job at a topless club in Roanoke and moved in with Steve, the bartender. He was pretty good to me. Sometimes, if his shift was bad, or his ex-wife called, he'd take up a drink and then he'd get kindly rough. But mostly he was nice. All the other girls was real jealous. I figured I was lucky.

I tried calling Momma once to let her know I was okay, but she wouldn't accept the charges. I heard her tell the operator she didn't have no daughter.

I missed my time of the month in July, but didn't tell Steve right away. When I did, he said how did I know it was his and when could I move my stuff out and by the way men don't want no pregnant waitress in a titty bar. And that was it.

So I called Momma again, but this time I yelled over the operator, "I'm pregnant, Momma," and she accepted the charges. She didn't like it none, but what could she say—*the apple don't fall far from the tree?*

I reckon Momma figured she'd get me back home and I could raise the baby living with her and Granny. As Steve would've said, "Fun city." I decided it didn't hurt nothing to let Momma think that for a while, but the day I come home I said, "Listen here, Momma, all's I need is $200 and a ride to the clinic." You should a seen her face.

Well, Momma lit into me right good. She said I'd be killing my baby, and where did I think I would be now if she'd had one of them things. She said I'd face God's wrath and maybe go to Hell and that my sinning got me in trouble and sinning again weren't the answer. I started to feel like Mary Magdalene, Salome, and Lot's wife all rolled into one.

Still, I got as far as the clinic before the worst of it hit. There was people there toting signs and handing out pictures of dead babies. This big old sweaty fat man stuck his face right in mine and yelled, "Murderer!"

One girl my age threw her body down on the sidewalk in front of me and yelled, "Don't do it!" Then I swear she started speaking in tongues of fire. Lord, didn't nothing make sense. Can you imagine people acting like that? You'd think it was their baby I was trying to get rid of.

After that, I told the clinic folks I didn't want them vacuuming up my baby. I'd clean up my own messes, thank you very much. Then I drove around for the longest, thinking on life, and how I come to get mine. I knew I wasn't like them crazy folks at the clinic, but still it just didn't seem right, that *operation.*

Not that being big as a house feels all that right, either, but I just plumb couldn't go through with it at the time.

So Granny and I went over to that new superstore in Christiansburg and put a crib on layaway. Momma's happy as a bug, and that's real nice. I got excited the other day, too, when Momma carried me to the doctor. He rubbed this thing over my belly and I seen my baby up on a TV screen. Its little fist was all tiny white shadow bones, like rock candy on a string. My sweet sugar baby.

It ain't exactly the virgin birth, but it'll do.

still life with shoes

Cecie was nursing her infant son when she got the call. Rich took off down the hall to answer it, and when he came back in and looked at her—wearing that tell-me-what-to-do expression that rearranged his whole tough Army face—and said there was someone on the phone, something about her dad, she knew. But even though she knew, her first thought was, *No. Impossible.*

The last time they'd spoken his voice had been so strong over the phone. They'd talked for an hour, discussed the baby, the joys and trials of parenthood, of life. On the other end of the line he'd sounded warm and deep, and—*dare she say it?*—fatherly. She'd gotten off the phone feeling buoyed and light; this after years of absorbing late night drunken soliloquies repeated until she herself could recite them: "Cecie, daughter of my heart, fruit of my loins. You. You alone are my hope for greatness. You are my immortality."

She'd never asked her siblings if they got similar calls, suspecting that they didn't. She would be the one he would call, she who loved, despite the drunken waste of life, she who could never hang up on him, could never tell him in the light of day what he had been the night before.

Cecie handed the baby to Rich and walked into the bedroom to take the phone, stumbling slightly as she rounded the corner at the end of the darkened hallway. She and Rich had lived in cramped

Fort Knox housing ever since the Army moved them there in her eighth month of pregnancy. How she had struggled to unload those big boxes, leaning down into them over her vast pregnant stomach, straining to get the last paper-wrapped treasure that she'd suddenly rather burn than try to find a spot for in their overflowing quarters.

She picked up the phone and held it to her ear. A ragged breathing sucked at her through the line. She could hang up now. She could.

"Hello?" she said instead.

"Yes! Oh, God. Is this Cecie? I'm so sorry. God, I never thought! And now, well never. Just never. You know? I mean, not him. Not *him*."

"I'm sorry?" she said. "Who is this?"

"Oh, Cecie, God. *I'm* sorry. This is Donny." A dim face hovered before her: gauntly thin, unshaven, disheveled Donny. One of her father's former art students, a groupie holdout from the days when he had still managed to make it, sober, into work. Yes, it was coming back. She'd met Donnie several years ago in one or another of the ragged Richmond flats her father rented in The Fan district. Floyd Avenue? Hanover? Was that with wife number two, three, or during his post-marriage single days? She decided it was the latter. "Cecie, I found your number in his things. Oh God."

"What's happened, Donny? Slow down." She lifted her bare feet from the cold parquet floor, crossed them on the bed, and stared into the mirrored closet door. Her old black portfolio, spilling over with art school sketches and prints from engraving class, peeked out from under the bed, fuzzy clods of dust—what her father had termed "slut wool"—already gathered around its edges.

"Happened? Shit. He's dead's what's happened. Gone. Cecie, I'd have called if I'd known. He said it was bad beans, a bad stomach, a binge drunk, I don't know. He said he'd be fine as long as they hooked up the IV to a keg of Budweiser. You know, shooting the shit to the end. Same old Ernie. I thought he'd be fine."

"Where is he, Donny?" It seemed very important to ask the right questions. If she remained calm and got the facts, the room would stop its wild lurching, her palms would cease their slippery sweating, her voice would lose its silly quiver.

"Where? Shit. MCV, I guess, the fucking Medical College of Virginia with a goddamn tag on his toe, I expect."

The baby began to cry from the living room. She could hear Rich winding up, too, with his "What? What?" refrain, begging the baby to give him instructions. Rich did maintenance for the Army's light tank brigade—or *performed* maintenance, as he always corrected her. Like it was a Broadway play he was putting on instead of greasy coveralls. He lived by the acronym PMCS: Preventive Maintenance, Checks and Services and it galled him that the baby couldn't adhere to such a sensible system.

"Donny, have you called the others?"

"Others?"

"Alan or Barry? Julie? The other kids?"

"Oh, Jesus, no. I was lucky to find your number off an old phone bill—I knew he said you'd moved to Kentucky, only person there any of us called, that's for sure. It had to be you. Your number, I mean."

"Well, let me call them and get back to you, okay? Where are you?"

"What? Oh, I'm at the place. Where your dad and I have—I mean had—rooms. Christ."

"Okay. I'm going to call the others now, Donny." A drum roll of muffled booms echoed from the firing range and rolled across the intervening fields: ten-ton tanks blasting their targets, a perpetual, distant thunder. "Donny? I'm hanging up, now. Okay?"

"Christ."

⌘

The first call went to Alan. As the eldest, he liked to take charge of things, and as an EMT he was the logical first choice to be told of a death. His roommate answered and said that Alan was at his latest girlfriend's house. Cecie asked the roommate for the number then called there. It was a mistake, though, because once she told him, Alan did his closed-up-tight routine, pissed to have her call him when and where she did. He told Cecie he couldn't talk and he'd call her later, as if it were an inconvenience to have to think about putting their father in the ground.

She moved on to Barry, then, and couldn't believe him either. You spend years growing up with a person and think you know them, but no, Barry screamed like a girl. He dropped the phone, which clattered around in her ear, echoing through the line. It sounded like he was down inside a bucket, beating his chest and howling. She could hear Barry's little Korean wife trying to placate him in the background, then all of the sudden she'd picked up the phone and was asking, "What? What wrong? What the matter?"

Cecie had to look up Julie's number. Ever since she took up with that South American boyfriend cum common-law-husband of hers, whom it sure looked as if she was supporting, Jules and she hadn't had much to talk about. As it turned out, though, Jules was pretty good about the whole thing and she offered to make arrangements for a cremation, including payment, since their father was flat broke.

The rest of the evening was spent like this: calls back and forth between siblings, calls to the hospital to determine cause of death, calls to her pediatrician about flying with the baby, calls to her father's ten brothers and sisters, fifteen minutes for nursing the baby and sobbing, calls to cancel various upcoming appointments, and calls to the airlines.

By morning, the siblings had agreed to converge in Richmond, rent a van, pick up the ashes from the funeral home, and then drive their father's remains deep into the mountains of his birth.

⌘

In the front room of Osgood Funeral Parlor, Cecie handed the baby off to Julie who took him, stiff-armed at first, then high against her shoulder, jiggling nervously and circling the room even though he wasn't fussing. Barry strolled the perimeter examining the artwork on the walls, a series of neutral, somber still lifes with dark fruit piled in bowls. When the funeral director emerged from a back room, Alan stepped forward to take the box of ashes then quickly passed it to Cecie as if it might burn him. The box was square and solid, strangely heavy for its small size, yet strangely light when she considered the contents: a whole human. Cecie held the box away from her body. None of them looked at it.

Along with the box, the funeral director gave them an official death certificate and a bag containing the auxiliary remains of their father: his upper dentures, yellowed, and missing four teeth on the right side; his glasses, thick, old, and ambered, nose pads grimy with the grease of human existence; and an old, yellowed Timex with a cracked face and a stretched-out wristband. Even as she recognized them, it seemed impossible that these objects could have come from her father's body, that they could be—along with the box—all that remained.

At the van, Cecie had an itching and unreasonable desire to put the box into the baby's car seat and strap it in. Instead, she handed it to Barry who looked around helplessly until he finally said, "Here Dad, you sit here," and stowed the ashes under the seat.

Julie laughed, a harsh bark of a sound that startled the baby; he threw his arms out straight and his face crumpled into a long wail. Julie held him out to Cecie who lifted her shirt and brought him to her breast.

"Jeez, there isn't time for you to do that," said Barry.

"I can feed him in the car seat," said Cecie. "I do it all the time when Rich and I travel. Rich can't stand the crying, and he doesn't want to stop, so I climb in the back and twist around." She put the baby, still nursing awkwardly, into the car seat, interrupting him only long enough to pull the strap over his head.

"Don't you have a bottle?" asked Alan, looking away and climbing into the driver's seat.

"Jakey's only breastfeeding." Cecie adjusted her shirt to cover as much of her middle as possible and cranked her body to the side.

"Geez," said Julie, "what do you do when you leave him with someone?"

"I don't. He's only two months old."

"You don't think mom did that with us, do you?" said Alan.

"Good Lord, no," said Barry. "They laid Cecie out on the seat of the station wagon as a baby. I can still remember the time she rolled right onto the floorboard when dad stopped hard. Phyllis wasn't exactly the attentive type."

"*Phyllis?*" said Alan. "What's wrong with *Mom?*"

"She didn't earn that title. Anyway, Rachel says to use her name. She says I need that once-remove to keep the pain at bay." Barry looked out the window and pointed. "I love those old broken-down barns."

"Rachel?" said Alan.

"Barry's therapist," said Julie. "Bet she works hard for her money."

"We made it to adulthood, didn't we?" said Cecie. "We're here." She wasn't sure why she felt the need to defend their mother. She knew what Barry said was true. As kids, they'd all run wild. Cecie hadn't one single memory of her mother from childhood; no body connected to the hand that served her dinner, the hand that tore a brush through her tangled hair, the hand that tucked her in at night. Cecie's clearest mother-memory involved her standing at the screen door staring out into the dark looking for headlights, asking for the tenth time, "When is Mommy coming home?" and getting no reply.

"Yeah, we're here," said Julie. "No thanks to her. Dad was a better parent than she was and he was an alcoholic. He was the one who managed to keep us alive. He drove you to the emergency room when you ate those pokeberries, me when Mom set me in the window and I fell three stories down, and Barry when he drank the bleach. What did Mom do?"

"I don't remember."

"You don't remember because she wasn't there. Even when she was there she wasn't there."

"Motherhood is hard. She did what I'm doing for Jake—diapers, and spit-up and clothes and warm blankets and rocking and nursing."

"Mom didn't nurse."

"Okay, well, bottles, then. Even harder."

"Not really, someone else can give a bottle. I used to feed you, and then when you got old enough she propped you up with it. If it fell, she didn't even notice, because you wouldn't cry. You never did cry, Cecie. Why didn't you cry?"

A pain swelled in Cecie's throat and stung at her eyes. Why didn't she cry? An image of a hopeless baby, a baby who knew better than to waste energy, passed before her. She discarded it as too tragic. "Maybe because Mom wasn't that bad. Maybe I was happy."

Cecie wondered if she defended her mother simply because no one else did. But honestly, she couldn't imagine being a mother like her mom had been. She'd rejected that model even as a child with her dolls.

⌘

On the drive to 2216 Fourth Avenue, the flophouse-style apartment their father rented along with an odd assortment of fellow down-and-outers, Cecie thought about the conversations she'd had with her father over the past few weeks. He'd been clear-headed and sober, she was certain of it. They'd had philosophical discussions about parenthood and life, about becoming a mother and nursing her new son. He'd sounded so *together*, something she hadn't heard in his phone voice for years—maybe ever—and she'd found it heartening. Ernie had sounded like a father.

She'd called him the last two times specifically because she'd had nightmares in which he died. His response had been laughter. Don't worry, he said, I'm too stubborn, too mean to die.

Then she remembered his one quick line about "getting hold of a bad can of beans and having a little stomach trouble," but he assured her it had passed and he was fine. The first inkling of his eroding stomach, and she hadn't caught it. The hospital had told her—when she telephoned for the details—that Ernie was admitted complaining of acute stomach pains. He'd listed no next of kin. When the pains persisted, the hospital scheduled exploratory surgery. Upon opening his gut, they found his stomach riddled with holes. *Swiss cheese* was the intern's analogy; and all they could do was sew him back up. He never regained consciousness.

Alan parked the van along the street outside their father's apartment. They had a prearranged visit to sort through Ernie's personal effects. Donny met them at the door.

"This way," he said, strangely subdued after that first hysterical phone call. His dun-colored hair had the wispy look of a long overdue cut. His eyes were heavy-lidded and red, the pupils excessively small. Julie turned to help Cecie carry the baby, asleep in his carseat, and Donny led them up the dank stairs to a door at the top of the landing.

Their father's room turned out to be a closet. A large one, long and thin, with a tiny window, but a closet nonetheless.

"This was his room," Donny said with a sigh, folding his arms and sagging sideways into the doorjamb. Donny's grief hung about his shoulders like a shadowy skin. Cecie thought about Donny, living with Ernie, sharing the dailyness of making a life in a way that Cecie couldn't even remember. Maybe they had stayed up late at night, discussing art, life, music, her. A strange combination of guilt and jealousy washed over her, leaving her tongue feeling thick. She had last seen her father at her wedding, a year-and-a half before.

"Thanks, Man," said Alan, stepping forward and holding out his hand. He used the clasp to turn Donny, guiding him, elbow-wise, into the hall and patting him on the back. Alan shut the door and the four children stood shoulder-to-shoulder in their father's tiny cubicle.

"It smells like him," said Julie as she set the baby, in his seat, on the unmade bed.

"What? Unfiltered Camels and booze?" asked Barry. He pushed and smacked at the window in the tiny rectangular piece of wall at the end of the room.

"It won't open," said Alan. "Dad and I lived in a row house on Floyd Avenue. The closet windows don't open. Trust me."

Cecie remembered that house. Specifically she remembered being eight and taking a Greyhound bus, alone, from Roanoke to Richmond, to spend the weekend with Alan and Dad. Alan was 17. Barry, 15, had run away and was living God knows where, and Jules, only just a teenager, was with an aunt on their mother's side. Cecie remembered the cockroaches, and how they fled the oven, in swarms along the wall, when her father turned it on to cook the Shake-N-Bake pork chops he had planned as a special treat.

The children looked around the closet-room. Beside the bed sat a stack of letters from Cecie, evidence of her recent obsessive flurry of communication, inspired, she sees now, by becoming a parent herself. The baby's squinting, fisted, hospital picture sat propped up on a stack of cinderblocks beside her father's bed. In the closet they found a few shirts, a pair of shoes, the suit he wore to Cecie's wedding (bought just for that purpose—he had given her away with such touching nervous pride), but little else.

"Where are all his works of art?" Cecie asked.

"Works of art?" said Alan.

"His art," said Cecie. "All the sculptures and paintings that were around the house in Manakin."

"I'm with Alan," said Barry. "What art?"

Cecie looked from face to face. "The big, colorful paintings, the size of a wall almost—I remember one with green birds flying out of squares, and one of Mom in the butterfly chair. And the sculptures from wood where he left bits of bark, smoothed it all around, and cut out the knotholes. I loved those."

"Cecie, that stuff was crap," said Julie, touching her on the arm. "They were never finished. Dad never finished anything."

"That's not true," said Cecie. "I remember—"

"How about that huge orange monstrosity, that thing that plugged in, with layers of colored crepe paper over holes and blinking Christmas lights behind them?" said Barry. "God."

Cecie remembered begging her father to plug that in before bed, so she could watch from the couch as multicolored lights flashed through cut out shapes, glass objects, and the clear plastic of a pair of safety goggles.

"Yeah. I remember that," said Alan. "It was hideous."

"I wish I knew where they were now," said Cecie.

Julie looked inside the cinderblock holes by their father's bed and found his checkbook. Surprisingly, it had $578 in it. "Just about enough to cover the cremation," Jules said, closing it with a snap.

Alan took a William and Mary college shirt—one he had given Dad during Alan's own days at the school—that he found folded up on the floor beneath a rod for hanging clothes. "Don't know what I'll do with it," Alan said, but rolled it up and tucked it under his arm. "What about you, Bare?"

"I don't need anything," said Barry, gesturing at the ground with his hands. "I've got all this emotional baggage to remember him by."

"You know, you really should learn to pack lighter," said Alan. "At least get it down to a carry-on, man. For all our sakes?"

"You don't want *anything*?" Cecie asked.

"Jesus, Cec, look around. The man had *nothing*. At the end of his life, this was all there was."

"He had us," said Julie.

In the end Cecie decided to keep her father's old, black shoes, solid and utilitarian, scuffed to gray at the toe, rubber heels worn to an outward slant. As she held them she was reminded of dancing with her father that night in the cockroach house, after he had put in the pork chops and opened a second, then third beer—still mostly sober—holding hands, each ball of her foot resting on his instep, moving with his every move. How they had laughed and danced, ending with a high stepping, backwoods flatfoot number that had them both in hysterics.

Perhaps Cecie should take the shoes home and sketch them in homage. Like Andrew Wyeth's farm boots, she could capture the dignified pathos of a life, as seen through the feet.

As they filed out of the room, Donny appeared. With a pointed look, he handed Cecie a photo. "This was taken last fall," he said.

In the picture, her father sits at a picnic table, a 6-foot-2, skin-covered skeleton holding a drink—a body with the pinched look of tightly stretched, nicotine-tanned skin. His forearms have the same circumference from wrist to elbow—an impossibly long distance—in the manner of the piled bodies of Auschwitz. It is horrifying. He had always been thin. Cecie knew that. But this? He must have just stopped eating.

In his early post-third-divorce days, Cecie had brought him grocery bags of food when she was in college nearby, at VCU, only to have him angrily accuse her of charity, and of treating her old man like a kid. So Cecie switched tactics and ordered the neutral postal delivery of mail-ordered summer sausages, fancy jellies, crackers and blocks of cheese—delivered on birthdays and food-related holidays that might allow Ernie to eat and save face. Once he called to thank her for a slab of Baby Swiss and said it was the only thing he'd eaten all week.

It hadn't been enough.

"Hey, man," Alan said to Donny. "Got all we wanted. Wasn't much there."

"No," said Donny, "there wouldn't be. He was saving up to visit his new grandbaby."

⌘

Next they stopped by The Science Museum of Virginia. Their father worked for years in this building, once the majestic old Richmond train station, which Cecie had toured when she first brought Rich to meet her father. Ernie had taken them everywhere throughout the entire building, from a walk out on the flat roof, to the basement that had been the underground terminal where the trains arrived and departed. Ernie had been the museum's indispensable Jack-of-all trades, and worked for peanuts, but all through the tour he had outlined the museum's grand plans for the building. It suited her father, who clearly had the run of the place. He'd always been a man of big dreams: create a timeless work of art—a Madonna or a Thinker; write the great American novel; distill the human condition into one perfect poem; become immortal.

When Cecie was young, her father had taken her to work with him when he taught Art at Bainbridge Junior High. Before the start of school or between classes she would walk beside him, clutching his large pointer finger in her fist and taking four steps to his one, while he marched her around the halls to the principal and fellow teachers who made a fuss over her and good-naturedly ribbed him. *For such an ugly man, Ernie, you've got awful cute kids. You sure you're the father?*

To Cecie, her father had been handsome. She loved his long, thin, Dick Van Dyke physique, the way everyone turned to look when he spoke, and his bizarre sense of humor. He could recite long, narrative poems without missing a word: The Rime of the Ancient Mariner, Little Orphan Annie, The Highwayman. He adored her with a fierce, protective passion. He called her his golden child.

⌘

To save money, the siblings spent that night in their mother's Richmond condo. As she climbed out of the car, Cecie looked back at the box of ashes. "Should we take them in?"

"God, no," said Barry. "Leave 'em in here. I sure as hell don't want them next to me when I'm sleeping."

"They'll get really hot closed up in the car," said Cecie.

"Honey," said Julie, "they're *ashes*. Heat's not gonna hurt them."

Cecie looked at her sister, the shortest and darkest of the four children, the one with their mother's looks. "I guess not," she said and turned away. "Mom's not here?"

"She's in Florida," said Barry, "with her new man, Ole Whatshisname."

"Ralph," said Alan. "His name's Ralph. Apparently Mom likes men with nerdy names."

Barry got the air conditioning in the condo working, Alan took charge of ordering pizza, and Cecie went upstairs to nurse the baby in the spare bedroom.

"Want some company?" asked Julie, sticking her head around the doorframe.

"If *you* don't mind. Jakey's kind of a noisy eater."

"Nah. He's fine." Julie grabbed a tiny foot and shook it gently.

"You think you'll have kids, Jules?" Cecie cupped her hand around Jakey's fine, thin hair and watched him nurse.

"Huh. Not in this lifetime. Not after our model of family life."

"You could break the cycle," said Cecie. "It's what I want."

"Nah, motherhood's not for me. It's not in me." The baby pulled away at the sound of Julie's voice; he turned his head to study her.

"It could be, though. Maybe you won't know until you try." Cecie lifted Jakey and passed him to Julie. "Burp him?"

Julie propped the baby against her shoulder and began patting. "I've got my own stuff to do. Kids take up too much time."

"I can't stand it any more," said Cecie, getting up and moving to the door. "I've got to bring his ashes inside."

⌘

During the next day's long drive to Riner, Virginia, deep in the heart of the Blue Ridge Mountains, the siblings searched one another for childhood memories.

"I've got a funny one," said Alan. "Remember the time Dad drove us up beside a car full of people and had us all wave? We didn't know them from Adam, but we all waved like crazy and pretended to recognize them."

"Yeah," said Julie, "and as we drove away Dad said, 'They'll be up all night wondering who we were!'"

"A real laugh riot, Dad," said Barry.

"You liked it at the time," said Julie.

"Lighten up, Bare," said Alan. "We all suffered."

"Except Cecie," said Barry. "Cecie didn't suffer."

"I don't know," said Julie. "Whenever Dad yanked me up from the table, Cecie would cry and say, 'Don't hurt Jewie.' She was the only one who spoke up for me."

"'Cause she was the only one who wouldn't get the shit kicked out of her," said Barry.

Cecie kept silent. She'd heard this argument so many times; she had nothing to add. As the youngest by five years, they didn't want to hear what she had to say anyway. Their truths had long been hashed out amongst themselves. There was no room for Cecie's interpretation.

And truthfully, Cecie didn't remember defending Julie. But she did remember her father in that belligerent stage of drunk, initiating an on-the-floor wrestling match with Alan, before dinner in the Floyd Avenue house, in order to prove he could still out-man his eldest son. She remembered that horrible helpless feeling, watching them roll around, laughing at first, then sensing Alan's rising anxiety and her father's single-minded power-lust, ending in the humiliation and ultimate full-body pinning of Alan, too roughly, for too long.

"Everything was shit," said Barry. "Everything."

"Oh, come on. We had *some* fun," said Julie. "You can't tell me nothing good ever happened. What about sledding behind the Simca?"

"Nothing," said Barry, and Cecie knew he meant it. Barry hated his wife, his job, his family, everything, with a heavy, indignant passion. Why should his childhood be any different? "Listen. Dad was an asshole when he was alive. He was fucked up, and he fucked me up. And I'm supposed to forgive him just because he's dead?"

"God. You are so angry." Cecie said this with awe. She had tried to summon that same sense of being wronged, of being cheated out of a normal childhood. She had tried to gather some giant force of fury, to explode unexpectedly. She thought there should be some righteous indignation in her somewhere, but there wasn't. And she couldn't.

"Saint Cecie," said Barry. "You know that unselfish love shit you always pull is a fault, too. It's called enabling. You being the perfect child didn't do Dad any good. He still drank himself to death. At least I tried to make him stop."

"By what? Running away?" said Julie. "Alan is the real saint, here. The patron saint of alcoholic puke."

"So," said Alan, turning the vehicle into a sharp curve; Cecie felt the car seat shift against her side. "Nice we're having weather. . ."

⌘

Since Ernie had no church affiliation, a borrowed minister interred their father. He mispronounced the family name and no one corrected him. In order to avoid paying for a plot, they buried Ernie's ashes in the old family cemetery between the graves of his mother and his mother's mother. Alan dug the hole and Cecie poured him in. It wasn't even a true plot, but it was free, the farmer who owned the land didn't care, and it sat on a small rise with a great view of the tin-roofed farming town where her father grew up. It seemed fitting.

As the first shovelful of dirt descended, Cecie darted forward and lifted a handful of her father's ashes; she let them sift between her fingers. They felt like gritty velvet air and left a haze of gray upon her palm. She didn't know where to wipe it.

Ernie's brother Bill stepped forward and guided her away from the grave. He put his arm around her. Uncle Bill could be her father's twin, except he looked ten years younger than Ernie, when in fact he was four years older.

"How do you do it?" Cecie asked, meaning *look so young.*

After a long silence, Uncle Bill said, "Honey, your dad got rode hard and put up wet. It just showed."

⌘

Something about the softness in Uncle Bill's voice made Cecie want to cry. And she remembered that moment—the pork chop moment—sitting with Alan at the rickety card table there in the house on Floyd Avenue. The chops were done and the second six-pack started and her father was gone. In his place was a man whose mood had sped past tipsy, through belligerent, and into insensate. He sat with his long legs folded under the card table and stared at the plates of food he had struggled so hard to produce. The knife slipped sideways when he cut his pork chop, so he picked the meat up in his fingers. His head sagged deeply over his plate, and his upper body swayed. The ends of his hair brushed the food on his plate.

Cecie looked at Alan. She had always fallen asleep before this.

"Drunk," mouthed Alan, and he stepped into the kitchen and out the back door. He came in with the second six-pack, popped the top of each remaining can, and poured it down the sink.

Alan returned to his seat and slipped an extra pork chop onto his father's plate undetected, then stuck his tongue out and poured milk into Ernie's beer. Ernie muttered into his plate and Alan said, "What Dad? What did you say?"

Ernie lifted his head with obvious effort and stared at eight-year-old Cecie with unseeing eyes. She realized then, that although she was only just witnessing it, this had been replaying every night for years. The thought made her feel loose-jointed and panicky, as if her chair were floating, suspended over a great valley, wind sucking at her ankles.

The pork chop moment was the moment she learned that grown-ups aren't always in control. That sometimes you have to do for yourself, and them, too. If she had that moment to live over, she would have cut his meat for him, made him eat, ushered him to bed. But instead she laughed. It wasn't like the dancing laughter. It was a laugh that felt short and wrong, a laugh that got stuck, that lodged in her chest and hurt.

The next afternoon, while unloading bags at the airport rental car return, Cecie found her father's shoes still tucked neatly under the rear seat. She had forgotten them and now her suitcase was full and it was past check-in time and the baby was fussing. She thought about discarding them, but couldn't, so she shoved them into the diaper bag where they poked out of the zippered top.

⌘

Cecie sits on the bed of her Fort Knox quarters, home again. She nurses the baby and stares at the shoes sitting atop her dresser, where they will stay, until she gets the chance to draw them.

She stares at the tattered black laces, the unevenly worn, turned-down heels (tangible evidence of her father's slight bow-legged step), and the dust-lined, feathery creases that travel across the instep, a sketch of passive information like the map of a palm. These shoes have seen a lot of wear. They sit on Cecie's dresser, ordering space like a sculpture, a three-dimensional still life. They are the emotional flipside of bronzed baby shoes, commemorating, rather than the rise of a life, the decline of one.

She has a sudden urge to try them on. She could see what it feels like to stand where he stood, feel the imprints of his feet beneath hers. She could be a child again, sliding her small feet into the vastness of her father's shoes, feeling the power and weightiness of them, joyfully mimicking the heavy shuffle clomp of his tread as she pushes her feet from room to room. She could remember still, her father laughing, holding his sides and gasping for breath, as he watched her stagger around the house, struggling to lift each foot, wearing her nightgown, his shoes, and the self-possessed smile of accomplishment. She had made him laugh.

Cecie lays her now-sleeping son across the bed, bolstered by pillows, and lifts the shoes from her dresser. She wonders what it must have been like, being Ernie. How he had managed to face each day, going to his job, pretending, yet surely knowing how every day would end. Getting his phone bill every month and seeing ninety-minute conversations that he could not recall, wondering what had been said.

Someday Cecie will have to figure out what to tell her son about his grandfather. Perhaps she will tell him her father was an artist, a man of many dreams and desires, a man who wanted to make a difference. But for today, she can still say nothing.

Cecie holds the dusty shoes against her stomach. Like the ashes, they are heavier than expected. And they are just shoes, nothing special, nothing noteworthy. But somehow it's the commonplaceness of them that soothes her. Just her father's shoes, her father's shoes and nothing more.

Cecie misses him. Pained and tortured and flawed as he was, she misses him. She sets the battered shoes on the floor and slides her feet into them. The contours of her father's feet rise and press into the bare soles of her own. The feeling is awkward and unsettling, but she is determined to be with him in this small way—she will wear what he had worn, stand where he had stood, feel what he had felt.

She will walk a mile.

Acknowledgments

First and foremost, I would like to thank my publisher and editor extraordinaire, Kevin Watson, for making this whole experience as fun and exciting as it could possibly be—and for treating me every step of the way as a professional collaborator and not "just the author." Also, I would be remiss, if in the same breath I didn't mention Sheryl Monks, Kevin's hardworking and very creative former business partner, who helped get this wonderful venture off the ground.

Thank you to my good friends—and excellent writers—Cliff Garstang and Tom Lombardo, who saw every one of these stories at some stage of their creation. To Tom I owe a special debt of gratitude for the collection's title—and, hey, it only took me three years to accept it.

I've been blessed to have a lot of good eyes on these stories over the years. I hope you will indulge my list. First, I want to thank my many writing friends and colleagues at the Zoetrope Writers' Studio, among them, Laila Lalami, Kirsten Menger-Anderson, Jim Tomlinson, Ron Currie, Jr., Katrina Denza, Myfanwy Collins, Alicia Gifford, Maria Robinson, Jim Ruland, Kelly Spitzer, Xujun Eberlein, Bev Jackson, Rusty Barnes, Anne Elliott, and Kay Sexton.

My in-the-flesh writing group has also offered invaluable suggestions and support: Hallie Block, Elizabeth Glenny, Ann Goldsmith, Joy Herrick, Helen Weiser, Anne Creaven, Carolyn Epes and Carol Keeney.

Ditto, my "big four" MFA instructors: Elizabeth Strout, Jonathan Dee, Susan Perabo and Naeem Murr, as well as Fred Leebron and Michael Kobre who run an excellent program. Also from my MFA program, the outstanding readers Lu Livingston, Susie Lawson, Claudine Guertin, Nancy Pinard, Pam Pearce, Priscilla Cutler, Carol Peters, Karen McBryde, Amy Smith Grigg, Rosie Dempsey, Gwynyth Mislin, Rosie Jones, and Susan Woodring.

Thanks to Jenn Rhubright for the use of her most excellent photo for the cover. And to *The Crazy River Think Tank* for all of the brainstorming, support, and love—especially Sonya St. Jacques and Kristin Beeler who brought us all back together after so many years.

I'm grateful to Michael Collier and Noreen Cargill at The Bread Loaf Writers' Conference, as well as my fellow social staffers Ru Freeman, Paul Yoon, and Sasha West. Thank you, also to Nina McGonigley for the germ of an idea that generated *Pygmalion (Recast)*.

For many and various reasons over the years (friendship, close readings, and emotional support among them) thank you to Paula Bolte, Dawn Estrin, Belinda Vidaurri, Kathy Helfrich, Darcy Daw, Carolyn Green, Margot O'Connor, Elaine Ragsdale, and Kim Rushing.

And last but in no way least, a big thank you to my family, who have offered their love and support and close reads for many years: my siblings, Sarah, Helen and Tyler; my mom, Sally Johnson; my father, Frank Akers; my children, Charlotte, Cady (Tomato!), and Scott; and my husband Len, who claims he doesn't "get" short stories, but reads them for me anyway and always has good suggestions.

Mary Akers
January 2009

About the Cover Artist

Jenn Rhubright's photography is of the most artistic variety. She captures not only the spirit of her subject, but also the unique environment in which it is found. The balance and composition engraved in her works are breathtaking. With an eye toward contrast and deeply saturated color, she creates images that are at once stunning and majestic. She has found muse in many photographic subjects from nature to landscapes, but has a special reverence for the classic American automobile, a subject that she has embraced with her full creative spirit. See more of Jenn's work at www.jennrhubright.com.

Printed in the United States
147044LV00001B/33/P